MARGY
MISUNDERSTOOD

MARGY
MISUNDERSTOOD

MARGARET SMITH

Margaret Smith

Margy

Maxwell Macmillan Canada

Maxwell Macmillan Canada
1200 Eglinton Avenue East, Suite 200
Don Mills, Ontario
M3C 3N1

Canadian Cataloguing in Publication Data
  Smith, Margaret (Margaret V.)
    Margy misunderstood

ISBN 0-02-954249-9 (bound) ISBN 0-02-954254-5 (pbk.)

I. Title

PS8587.M57M3 1994 jC813'.54 C94-930585-5
PZ7.S55Ma 1994

Cover Illustration: Greg Ruhl
Cover Design: Brant Cowie

Excerpts from "The Shooting of Dan McGrew" by Robert Service © 1910 Dodd Mead & Co. Reprinted by permission of Estate of Robert Service.

Printed and bound in Canada
1 2 3 4 5 98 97 96 95 94

♾ Printed on Acid Free Paper

This book is for
Mary and Jeremy
my first and finest works,
who for some years
lived in Margy's Fine House
in Bancroft.

CHAPTER
——1——

A tingle of excitement swept the class. One by one every single student turned and stared out the tall windows of Room Six.

Snow for Christmas!

And not one of those brief, timid, here-this-afternoon-gone-by-suppertime flurries. No, this was the out-and-out storm that had threatened for days, and now closed in over the village with a sudden violent fury of whistling wind and icy snowflakes that stung against the windowpanes.

Margy, in her seat at the front of the row nearest the windows, had a wonderful vantage of the glowering tumult. She pushed her glasses up on her nose, rested her chin in her hand and peered out, the outline map of Africa in front of her forgotten.

By now the snow would be drifted up against Daddy's old farmhouse in Manitoba, the tops of the fence posts almost lost beneath the wide drifts that blew before the icy winds. But here it was, less than two weeks before her first Christmas in Ontario, and up until now the village had still lain dry and brown.

Margy smiled out at the storm. Already the window sill was covered and white triangles were building up in the corners of the panes. Who cared about the "mean summer temperature" of Rhodesia when the first truly serious December storm of 1932 had arrived in Bancroft.

At the excited rustling behind him Mr. Warren turned from the blackboard where he had been writing the next day's arithmetic problems. He glanced out the window, sighed resignedly, and snapped the tattered map of the world beside him. It rolled reluctantly up on its spindle.

"Class," said the teacher briskly, "Christmas is only two weeks away. It's time to organize our gift exchange."

Mr. Warren took a large pair of scissors from the drawer of his desk and snipped a sheet of paper into thirty-two small squares.

"Now then," he said, "each person must sign his or her name on their slip of paper and we'll mix them up, and then each will select a person for whom to buy a gift."

It was kind of Mr. Warren to explain, thought Margy. It seemed to her as if the whole class had grown up and gone to school together forever. Even their parents and grandparents had known each other for generations. It was still difficult to be "the new girl," the one who had to have everything explained. Maybe by February, when Margy would have been in Bancroft for a whole year, life would be a little easier.

Mr. Warren distributed his scraps of paper and then retrieved his own hat from the hook behind the door.

"Write your name so that it may be clearly understood," he cautioned, "and as usual tell no one whose name you have drawn. This will be a secret gift from a Secret Friend."

Margy printed "Marguerite Stratton" on her scrap of paper in straight round letters, and then on the other side of the paper wrote "Margy Stratton," just to be sure.

As his hat went around the room collecting the folded scraps, Mr. Warren asked, "Now then, what limit shall we set on the cost of these gifts?"

"A nickel," two boys' voices chorused from the back of the room. That would be James (universally known as "Snuffy") and George. They always had a comment to make, seldom useful and never in earnest.

"A dollar!" This from Gwennie who sat in the front desk on the opposite side of the room from Margy. Gwennie was the only person in the class who always had extra pencils, and matching hair ribbons for each of her many dresses, and treats when it wasn't even her birthday.

"That, Gwenneth, might be a bit excessive," said Mr. Warren. "Let's hit a mid-point, say, fifteen cents." Margy, who was excellent in arithmetic, knew that fifteen was scarcely midway between five and a hundred, but there was a murmur of agreement through the classroom and so it was settled.

Margy was the last to drop her paper in the hat. Mr. Warren mixed the slips well before he started the hat around again. This time each student took a name out.

Gwennie was the first to draw. She unfolded her slip of paper, looked momentarily annoyed, then quickly simpered as if she had drawn the best name in the whole room. Margy had no doubt but that she had.

The hat went up and down the aisle. As each

person unfolded a slip, he or she reacted with a smile or a groan, with a pleased look or a roll of the eyes. George and Snuffy, who sat beside one another at the back of the room, each peered into the hat before they drew, then selected a slip carefully, read it, and silently shook hands across the aisle. So much for "secret" thought Margy.

Finally it was her turn to draw a name. Being the very last she expected only one slip left in the hat, but surprisingly there were three. Margy took one out and passed the hat back to Mr. Warren. He appeared to take no notice of the two remaining scraps of paper, but as he hung his hat back behind the door Margy saw him slip them into his waistcoat pocket. She glanced around the room to see if anyone else had witnessed the teacher's action. But every face in the room was watching her expectantly, waiting to see her open her slip of paper. Every face, that is, except those of two boys over at the side of the room whose eyes were cast down at their desk tops.

They appeared to be studying their Africa maps intently, thirteen-year-old Orlie Marker in Senior Fourth with Margy and his younger brother Cline in Junior Fourth. They came from a sprawling dirt-poor farm family just out of the village. This "Great Depression" that the whole country was suffering under had been particularly tough on families like theirs. Even fifteen cents would be well beyond their means. Somehow the two brothers must have managed to only pretend to draw a slip from the hat as it went by.

Margy did not wish to open her slip of paper in front of all those prying eyes. She folded her tall skinny frame into as small a space as possible and hunkered down over the little white scrap.

Fortunately at that moment Mr. Warren said in a back-to-business tone, "You have four minutes to tidy your desks before you leave for home. I shall let you out five minutes early because of the storm."

This drew everyone's attention back to the delightful fact of the snow and there was a scramble as they dove into their desks, straightening and sorting. Margy did not tidy her desk. She was busy unrolling the slip of paper in her hand. Please let it be someone nice, she prayed inwardly. It would be too much to hope that she would be lucky enough to draw Lenore Spenser, or Verna Cooper, Margy's Best Friends. And oh dear, what if it were Gwennie!

Cradling the slip of paper in the privacy of her lap, Margy pushed her glasses straight with her finger and read the name.

Ralph Phillips.

Margy blinked her eyes and read it again. It still said Ralph Phillips, printed in the self-same straight letters with the curly "R" that she had seen him use so often when he was sent to work on the blackboard.

She glanced carefully over her shoulder to where Ralph sat at the back of the room near George and Snuffy. Ralph the handsome, with the dark hair and bushy eyebrows. Ralph the kind, always ready to include a younger kid in a baseball game or tug-of-war. Ralph the funny, at the centre of any diversion in the classroom and who had written more lines than anyone else in the Fourth Form with the possible exception of Snuffy Farrow.

Ralph. And Margy had his name for the gift exchange. She folded her precious slip of paper and tucked it inside her spelling book ready to take home.

At exactly three fifty-five Mr. Warren said, "You may be dismissed. And don't forget to bring your donation to the community Christmas Cheer Fund tomorrow."

The class rose and sang "God Save the King" with rather more enthusiasm than usual, and there was a general stampede to the coat hooks at the back of the room. The boys pressed out the door, eager to get out into the snow for the first really decent snowball fight of the season. The girls lingered around the coat hooks, buttoning up slowly and pulling on mittens.

"Whose name did you get?" whispered Lenore at Margy's ear. Without waiting for a reply, she went on, "I got Jane." Lenore looked pleased. Jane was the quieter of the Parker twins, both in Senior Fourth, neighbours of Lenore and Margy and members of their secret club, The Order of the White Cloud.

Verna slid up to the two girls and hissed, "Lenore, you're not supposed to tell." Then in the same breath, "I got Amy Lawson. Whose name did you get, Margy?"

Before Margy could figure out a way to get out of telling, Gwennie barged into the whispered conversation. She adjusted the fur collar of her coat just so and said sweetly, "Well, of course we're not supposed to say who we got so I'll just give you a hint: he's the best-looking boy in the whole Senior Fourth and he sits right at the back . . . and his initial is 'R.'"

Verna and Lenore let out an appreciative sigh. Margy hugged her spelling book closer to her chest and said nothing.

It took only a minute for Margy to get home. She lived in the house just next door to the school. It was a fine house, brick and solid, built by her Grandfather many years ago. Her Momma had grown up in the Fine House, and living there made Margy feel closer to Momma than she had since Momma died, four and a half years earlier. Momma and Grandfather and the Fine House had always stood for "safeness." And now it was Margy's home, ever since she had come from Daddy's farm in Manitoba almost a year ago to live with Aunt Alice and Aunt Edith.

Margy loved the Fine House. Going up the broad front walk and through the big front door was something like going into a strong castle where one could feel warm and protected no matter what the outside world did to her.

Not that Grandfather was still there either. No, he had died three years earlier in 1929, right after "The Crash" that had started this terrible Depression. But Aunt Alice was there in the Fine House. Aunt Alice who was small in stature, but strong and practical and smart and independent. Oh yes, Aunt Edith was there too. It was Aunt Edith who could fill the house with inviting aromas, like pumpkin muffins or maple syrup cake fresh from the oven, and it was Aunt Edith who was so soft and tender-hearted that she would burst into tears when she had to put a mouse trap under the kitchen sink. But it was Aunt Alice who made the Fine House feel like *home*. With her "at the helm" Margy knew that nothing much could go wrong.

The two Aunts were in the kitchen at the back of the house, as they usually were at this time of day. The simple suppers they ate were not so elaborate as to require much preparation, but somehow both Aunts always seemed to be in the kitchen when Margy came home, waiting to hear about her afternoon at school, or any news from the village that she might have picked up at recess. Aunt Edith, the younger of the two, went out very seldom. She had "terrible bad legs," as she said, and even to walk down the hill to church each Sunday was an effort. Aunt Alice also confined her outings, aside from three afternoons a week in the village library at the community centre, to a trip down street once a week for special errands. So they both depended on Margy for whatever news she could pass along. And Margy was always eager to give them the latest, sometimes enhanced with fanciful detail, as she ate her after-school snack.

"We drew names this afternoon," she said importantly, between bites of a juicy apple. "Everyone will get a gift from a Secret Friend." She licked her lips for an elusive drop of apple juice. "But we mustn't spend more than fifteen cents."

"Fifteen cents!" Aunt Alice was shocked. To her sister she said, "There must be lots of children in the class for whom fifteen cents would be a small fortune."

Margy told Aunt Alice about the two slips left in the hat after it had gone all around the room the second time, and about Orlie and Cline Marker who looked so quiet and sullen.

"Whose name did you draw, dear?" asked Aunt Edith.

"Oh, just a boy in the class," said Margy carelessly, taking a large bite of apple to discourage requests for further details. The Aunts knew Ralph and his mother because they all went to St. John's Church together.

"Well, you'll just have to think of something nice to buy him," said Aunt Edith, "unless you want me to make him a big batch of peanut brittle."

Yes, I will have to think of something really swell, thought Margy. But not peanut brittle, not even Aunt Edith's special peanut brittle with so many nuts in it that it looked like lace and just about melted in your mouth. No, Ralph's gift would have to be something permanent, something lasting, something that he would keep and cherish forever. Choosing something like that would take a lot of thought, but not now. Later, when she was alone.

"Auntalice," Margy said aloud to change the subject, "everyone in the class is supposed to bring a donation for the community Christmas Cheer Fund. This will provide," (she was unconsciously parroting Mr. Warren's earlier explanation), "a hamper of food, clothing, and a toy for every needy family in our community." She stopped abruptly because she suddenly remembered hearing something about this on Sunday at church during the rector's announcements. No doubt the Aunts already knew all about this. They actually listened to the announcements in church.

"That's fine, Margy," said Aunt Alice. "You take out of your money box whatever you think you should give, and I'll donate as well. In fact, I have just the thing."

She retrieved her handbag from the stand in the front hall and rummaged around in the bottom for her coin purse.

"There," she said triumphantly. "I knew it was in here. I was saving this for something special." She produced a coin and handed it to Margy. It was a quarter dollar, but not an ordinary one. No indeed, it was a bright and shiny American quarter.

Margy turned it over and over in her hand. "Look," she said excitedly. "It says 1919 on it, just the same year as I was born. This quarter is exactly the same age as I am. I wonder what the chances are that it was made on September seventeenth."

"Rather slim, I expect," said Aunt Alice drily. "Still, it is interesting to speculate."

Margy nodded agreeably, even though she wasn't sure what "speculate" meant. She thought there was a sign in the lobby of the Queen's Hotel on Hastings Street that asked gentlemen not to do it in public.

"And Margy," continued Aunt Alice, "most of the students won't be able to give that much money to the Christmas Cheer Fund, so don't you make a big show of it. Just slip it in quietly when no one is looking."

Margy nodded and went to put the special quarter deep into the pocket of her school coat so she wouldn't forget it in the morning. Then she went upstairs to her little room and dumped her money box out on her bed. One quarter, one dime, three nickels and thirty-two pennies. (She kept the silver half-dollar her Grandfather had given her in a sock under her mattress all by itself, and did not include it in her spending money at all.)

Eighty-two cents. Margy moved the coins around in little piles on the crazy quilt. Gift for Aunt Alice, twenty-five cents; gift for Aunt Edith, the same (so her feelings wouldn't be hurt); gift for Lenore, five cents; gift for Verna, the same (so *her* feelings wouldn't be hurt); gift for Ralph, fifteen cents; donation to the Christmas Cheer Fund, seven cents. But what about Mr. Warren? Some kids in the class were giving him a gift. And what about Jane and Cora? What about Snuffy and George and . . . . So many friends, she thought. Should I be giving all these people gifts? It was hard to know what people did at Christmas here in Bancroft. Back out west gifts were confined to immediate family.

Margy thought with satisfaction of Daddy's gift which she had already sent off. It was a dandy too, a small scoopy-looking tool for cleaning his pipe. Aunt Alice had said that it must be in the post by "half-past November" in order to make sure it reached Daddy before Christmas, so Margy had mailed it right after Armistice Day. She did *not* send a gift for Daddy's new wife or her baby, Margy's half-brother who would be celebrating his first Christmas in Daddy's little farmhouse on the prairie.

The next day right after school Margy took all her money and went on a shopping expedition. Within half an hour she was back, broke but triumphant. Now in place of the small piles of money her purchases were spread out on the crazy quilt where she could admire them.

First of all for Aunt Alice, a nice box of stationery, cream-coloured with matching envelopes (twenty-eight cents). It wasn't a big box but Aunt Alice could save it for Special Correspondence. Next, a fine box of dusting powder for Aunt Edith (twenty-five cents). It was an oval box with a satiny feel to the paper cover, and had its name, "Lilacs in the Moonlight," printed in gold letters on the bottom. Margy knew that Aunt Edith liked lilacs; in the spring she filled the house with their fragrant blooms from the lilac hedge in the backyard.

And finally, and best of all, Ralph's gift.

Margy had been at a loss for what to buy Ralph, but Mr. Rainer at the hardware store where she had done all her shopping was most helpful.

"Gift for a boy, eh, Margy?" he mused, rubbing his stubbly chin. "Cousin, maybe? . . . Well, let's see now." His eyes ranged along the shelf behind the counter. Suddenly they lit up and he reached for a small box at the very end, half-hidden behind some packages of chewing tobacco. "Now, here's exactly what you want, lass, and because it's you, I'm marking 'em down from thirty cents to twenty cents."

He wiped a layer of dust off the box with his plaid sleeve and opened it up on the counter. Inside were a pair of men's braces. But what a pair of braces! They were bright scarlet with shiny gold fittings and neat black leather loops at the bottom to attach to the gentleman's trousers.

"There you go," said Mr. Rainer heartily. "The perfect gift. Make any man stand out in a crowd. Probably the only pair like it in the county. And here I was saving them for somebody special. I'm sure glad you happened along, Margy, before someone else snapped them up."

They were wonderful braces, and Margy felt sure that Ralph would love them and keep them forever. And if she skimped on her other purchases she could just manage it. She had bought them on the spot before Mr. Rainer could change his mind. Now she sat on her bed and examined them again before she wrapped them up. They were absolutely splendid.

She retrieved the box of tissue paper from the hall cupboard and wrapped her gifts, each in a different colour: white for Aunt Alice, green for Aunt Edith, and red for Ralph. Lots of bright Christmas stickers secured the ends of the packages, and when she was finished they all three looked inviting and festive.

The next week was a whirlwind of activity in the school, in the community at large and in the Fine House. There were Christmas tests to study for, final rehearsals for the School Concert and the Church Concert, and special choir practices to work up the carols for the Christmas Eve service. Then there was all the extra baking and preparations for drop-in visitors and Christmas dinner. (Aunt Alice had invited Uncle Howard and Aunt Clara, as well as the organist at the church, a spinster lady who didn't have a family close by with whom to celebrate Christmas.) There was popcorn to pop and string, and then the tree itself to find and set up and decorate.

Margy had thought they would simply go for a walk in the bush a few minutes from home and cut a tree. But Aunt Alice was not in favour of killing one more tree than necessary and decreed that they would just wait until the trees from the schoolrooms were discarded and reclaim one of those. Besides, Aunt Alice was very picky about Advent being Advent, and Christmas not beginning until sundown on December twenty-fourth, so waiting to use one of the old school trees was just fine.

Finally, there was the important choice of which of her stockings Margy would select to hang on her bedpost. She would have liked to hang up one of her long brown stockings, but that might have appeared greedy, so she settled on using one of the pretty blue bedsocks that Aunt Edith had knit for her birthday in the fall. Margy did, however, wear both socks on the same foot for several nights to maximize the stretching possibilities of the outer one.

At last, in spite of Margy's doubts to the contrary, Friday afternoon finally arrived. The scholars of Mr. Warren's forms had written their last test. The School Concert had been a tremendous success. The money collected for the community Christmas Cheer Fund had been securely sealed in a jar in Mr. Warren's bottom desk drawer, ready to be picked up over the holiday by Mr. Cooper, chairman of the School Board and one of the village councillors (and Verna's father).

Mr. Warren acted as St. Nicholas, passing out the lumpy parcels that had accumulated in the branches of the class Christmas tree. "You may open your gift right now," he said, "or take it home to place under your own tree."

Because one couldn't be sure whether one's Secret Friend might give a gift that was odd or embarrassing, everyone elected to take their gift home where it could be opened in privacy. Everyone did, that is, except Snuffy and George. They opened their gifts immediately. Snuffy received a dandy flashlight. George's gift was an identical dandy flashlight.

Margy's gift was beautifully wrapped in three different colours of tissue paper all layered together, with both Christmas stickers and ribbon. The card read, "Merry Christmas and Happy 1933 to Margy Stratton from her Secret Friend."

Margy watched out of the corner of her eye as Ralph went up to the tree to receive his gift. He examined the bright red package carefully and said, "Thank you, sir," to Mr. Warren. The teacher smiled back at him and said, "Happy Christmas, Ralph." Margy was relieved to see that everyone in the class received a gift from under the tree. Mr. Warren was indeed a kind man.

After school Margy handed out her other gifts. Aunt Edith had made a gigantic batch of peanut brittle and another of sponge toffee for Margy to divide among her friends. She had packets for Lenore, Verna, Jane and Cora (together), George and Snuffy (also together, which they immediately opened and ate), and for Ralph (just to throw him off the scent of suspecting who his Secret Friend might be).

Margy got gifts too. One from Lenore, another from Verna and a third one, very lumpy and a little on the grubby side, from George.

In spite of their eagerness to get home and start the holidays, a large group lingered in the schoolyard after dismissal. There was much to discuss regarding Christmas plans. The Church of England Concert was that evening and the United Church Concert the next. Everyone went to both, so they finally parted with shouts of "See you later!"

Margy walked slowly towards the Fine House. In the dusk a few flakes of snow were beginning to float down and the temperature was dropping rapidly. But Margy felt a warm glow that seemed to start from right inside her, the kind of feeling that comes with having friends and being a friend.

Margy thought back on this moment a few weeks later when the warm glow had turned to wet ashes.

CHAPTER
—2—

The first rays of Christmas morning light slivered across Margy's bedroom window sill shortly before eight. She lay curled in a tight warm ball under her crazy quilt and watched them for what seemed like an eternity.

Finally, leaning over and out of her bed, she scratched a small hole in the frost on her windowpane and peered out. The snow that had begun to fall again as they walked home from church after the midnight service now blanketed everything in a fresh mantle of sparkling white. The Grants' cosy house across the street with its small gables and stubby chimney looked like the picture on a Christmas card. Margy could see lights on in their parlour, and even caught a momentary glimpse of someone, probably Mickey, the youngest Grant, charging past the lighted window. No doubt they were enjoying their Christmas tree right this minute before they went off to Mass at eight o'clock.

Aunt Alice had explained the Christmas routine of the Fine House to Margy the night before. "We'll all go to the Christmas Eve service early tonight to be sure to get our own pew," she said. "And by the time we help tidy up the church and get home it will be after one o'clock in the morning. Now Margy, I don't want you popping out at the crack of dawn. Wait until you hear your Aunt Edith go down to put the chicken in the oven. We'll have our gifts off the tree after breakfast."

When Aunt Alice used that tone of voice there was no use arguing. But she went on, "There is, however, no reason why you may not look at your stocking as soon as you wake up. We," (she glanced at Aunt Edith), "were always allowed to do that." Margy thought, fancy Aunt Alice and Momma and Aunt Edith as little girls in pigtails, pantelettes and pinafores, hanging their stockings on their bedposts on Christmas Eves long past. It made a fascinating image.

Now Margy pulled herself out of the warm pocket in the middle of her bed and crawled to the foot where she untied the deliciously lumpy sock from her bedpost. Rather than turn on the electric light she pulled the quilt around her and up over her shoulders and sat on the bed by the window where the wintry sunlight was growing stronger by the minute.

She hesitated. Dump the stocking out all at once? Or reach in and savour the things one at a time? She opted for the latter.

Right on the top, a cunning little harmonica. Margy blew a cautious reedy note, then set the mouth organ on the window sill. Her hand dove into the sock again. Out came a packet of peanut brittle wrapped neatly in waxed paper. Margy opened it and took a bite. She grinned to herself and folded the packet shut, setting it on the window sill alongside the harmonica. Next, a pretty handkerchief with daisies embroidered around the edge. Then a beautiful round orange with its silky skin and pungent fragrance. Along the side was a new red toothbrush, and last of all, right in the toe of the sock, a hard brown Brazil nut.

Margy admired the array of gifts now displayed on the window sill. So many things and this was only the beginning. She hugged herself inside the rolled-up quilt in anticipation.

The day flew by like a golden butterfly.

Right after breakfast and even before they got properly dressed for the day, Margy and the two Aunts went into the parlour. Their reclaimed tree looked very festive with its fine spun-glass ornaments and the chains of popcorn and cranberries looped in stately array. The three sat facing the tree, the Aunts in chairs and Margy on the floor, and opened their gifts one at a time.

Aunt Edith loved her lilac dusting powder. Aunt Alice pretended to scold Margy and Aunt Edith for giving her gifts at all; she had said that she needed to buy new eyeglasses right after Christmas and that would be her gift from everyone because they would cost so much money. But she was pleased in spite of herself when she opened the stationery from Margy and the pretty black kid gloves from her sister. She looked rather strange sitting in the fine front parlour wearing her threadbare and patched old grey flannel dressing gown together with the dressy kid gloves, rather like a character out of a comedy pantomime.

Margy received wonderful gifts too. From Aunt Alice she got the latest Lucy Maud Montgomery book, *A Tangled Web,* with a leather cover and coloured plates. Aunt Edith gave her a lovely red cardigan sweater with a snowflake pattern that she had knitted herself, as well as a matching pair of mittens. Margy felt just the tiniest bit disloyal to Momma as she thanked Aunt Edith for the gift. Momma had always said that Margy couldn't wear red because of her red hair. But several people had commented lately how Margy's hair was darkening into more of an auburn, so perhaps it was all right now. Besides Aunt Edith must have worked long hours and always while Margy was away at school to keep it a secret, so the sweater was a very fine gift.

The gift from Margy's Secret Friend in Room Six turned out to be a box of dusting powder ("Merry Marigolds"), as did Verna's offering ("Roses in the Mist"). The gift from George was a hand-carved cat, or perhaps it was a mouse, although Aunt Alice said it was clearly a fox with a very thin tail.

They scarcely had time to clear up around the tree, straighten and flatten the tissue paper to be used again next Christmas, and put their gifts away before it was time to dress properly and get ready for their guests to arrive for dinner. In no time at all the little organist was at the door, followed closely by Uncle Howard and Aunt Clara, with Uncle Howard stamping the snow off his boots and demanding loudly, "Is this where the feast is at?"

And what a feast! There was roast chicken with sage and onion dressing, creamy mashed potatoes, turnips and carrots and green beans (all preserved from the Aunts' own garden), and cranberry jelly shimmering like rubies in its little crystal bowl. And gravy. Everything *drowned* in gravy. For dessert, a great plum pudding (why was it called plum pudding, thought Margy, when there didn't seem to be any plums in it) with both hard sauce and soft sauce to go with it.

Uncle Howard pushed back from the table and announced that he wouldn't need to eat a single thing more for three full days. The adults retired to the parlour for coffee and thick slabs of Christmas cake, brought as a "bread-and-butter" gift by the organist to thank the Aunts for inviting her to share their Christmas. Meanwhile, Margy cleared the table and stacked the dishes, carefully keeping aside all the chicken bones so that Aunt Edith could make soup the following week.

At two o'clock all activity ceased and everyone gathered respectfully around the radio in the parlour to hear the King give a Christmas greeting to his subjects. This was the very first time he had ever spoken to the whole empire in this way and it made Margy feel very important to be listening to the King speak to them in his very own voice all the way from England. After he finished his greeting the radio played "God Save the King" and "O Canada," and everyone stood to attention facing the radio. Uncle Howard, who had been in the Great War, saluted.

Then there was time for a quick dash to Lenore's house to swap Christmas news and admire gifts before Margy had to be back to help with the major clean-up after the guests departed.

It was a very good Christmas.

As Margy lay in bed that night she played the whole day over in her imagination, like a movie only in slow motion. She decided that the very best part was her beautiful new book from Aunt Alice. Practical Aunt Alice, who didn't even want a gift herself because she had to spend so much money on new eyeglasses. Unsentimental Aunt Alice, who nevertheless handled books with a kind of reverence most people reserved for holy artifacts or photographs of a lover killed overseas. Aunt Alice must have spent a great deal of money on that book, money scrimped from her meagre salary as the village librarian.

Margy had tried to thank her when she opened the gift, but somehow words seemed inadequate. She knew deep in her heart that the best way to thank Aunt Alice was simply to read the book and enjoy it and talk to her about it afterwards, and never to turn down the corner to mark her place, and *never* to leave her new book open flat, face down, and crack its spine. But even all that didn't seem enough. And remembering the scrawny little box of stationery she had given Aunt Alice, which had seemed so fine in the store, now made Margy's cheeks burn red in the dark.

Right there and then Margy resolved that next Christmas she would give Aunt Alice something so grand, so wonderful, that her Aunt would know, once and for all, how much Margy loved her. Yes, a gift for Aunt Alice: a sort of grand *beau geste* that Margy would save up her money for all year. She didn't know yet what the Wonderful Gift would be. Nevertheless, as she lay in the dark, and just before she said her prayers, Margy vowed that by the time she went back to school she would have decided exactly what she could give Aunt Alice next year for Christmas, so that she could start saving her money for it immediately. She mentioned Aunt Alice's Wonderful Gift to both Momma and God in her prayers and her resolve became a kind of Sacred Oath. Margy drifted off to sleep satisfied.

"Before she went back to school" had seemed like a lot of time to think about it and decide. But the crisp clear weather held and the whole holiday was crammed with activities: ice skating and tobogganing parties; bobsled races down the Flint Street hill in front of the school; taffy pulls and euchre parties; snowball forts and fights, and hockey matches with the boys down on Cow Bell Alley; the special Christmas movie at the theatre, Greta Garbo in *Grand Hotel* plus two cartoons and three newsreels. Then came the New Year's Eve party at Jane and Cora's, with Verna and even Lenore allowed to come, and they all stayed up until midnight and toasted the New Year in ginger ale.

Suddenly it was Saturday, the last shopping day before school started again. Margy knew that today was the day she must decide what Aunt Alice's Wonderful Gift was to be.

Providentially, at breakfast Aunt Edith asked Margy to go down street right after her Saturday chores were done and fetch some more grey wool to finish the socks she was working on for the church "bale."

"Mind you go to Cooper's Emporium now," cautioned Aunt Edith. "That's where I bought the rest. I'll give you a sample to take to be sure you buy the right colour."

Margy hugged herself inwardly. Cooper's Emporium was the "swankiest" shop in town, also the most expensive, much more exclusive than Rainer's Hardware Store where she had done all her Christmas shopping. That was indeed the best place in Bancroft to look for

Aunt Alice's Wonderful Gift. And here was a perfect excuse to go in and look around.

Margy flew through her chores and at eleven o'clock she was off, the dime for Aunt Edith's wool held carefully inside her new red mitten. She passed some of the boys sliding on the Flint Street hill. Ralph was there, all bundled up against the cold so Margy couldn't see if he was wearing the scarlet braces. And of course she couldn't ask him as that would give her away, so she merely waved back at them and continued on her mission down the hill.

She pushed the heavy door of the Emporium open. Inside the store it was toasty warm and smelled of Yardley's English Lavender soap. Mr. Cooper always brought in a large supply for Christmas, a popular gift for men to give their wives, so much more festive and romantic than an egg poacher or a dust mop.

As she closed the door a tiny bell above Margy's head tinkled and a rather severe-looking lady behind a counter halfway back looked up. Margy looked around the store carefully. It would be so much more fun to be "waited on" by Verna's older sister, or better yet, Verna herself, who was sometimes allowed to help out in her father's store on weekends. Alas, there was no sign of either, so Margy marched right up to the severe-faced lady and said, in a businesslike tone, "My Aunt would like to have one more skein of this wool, please."

The saleslady examined the sample Margy handed her and turned to the drawers behind the counter.

"And your aunt is . . . ?" she inquired over her shoulder.

"Miss Edith Mullett," said Margy quickly.

The severe lady's face cracked into a thin smile. "Oh yes, grey socks for the Church of England bale, right?"

Margy nodded. "She was just turning the heel and she ran out," she said, and then immediately wished she hadn't. Perhaps it would sound as though Aunt Edith didn't plan ahead properly, or that the saleslady had shorted her on the amount of wool in the last skein. The severe-faced lady however paid no notice to her remark.

She said, quite congenially, "You're the little girl that's visiting with the Mullett sisters, aren't you?"

"Not visiting—I live with them. For almost a year now." Margy wanted to add, "And I'm not a 'little girl.' I'm thirteen and a half years old." But she knew she shouldn't be what Aunt Alice would call "saucy."

"Yes, of course," said the saleslady smoothly. "Now, will there be anything else, dearie?"

"No, thank you." Margy hesitated. It would be best to get permission for her search for the Wonderful Gift. "Would you mind if I looked around your store for a few minutes? I'm searching for something special . . . but I don't know . . . what it is yet." Her voice trailed off lamely.

The severe saleslady's eyes ranged around the store and softened with pride, and she actually smiled. "You go right ahead, dearie. I'll just get your change."

Margy leaned on the counter and watched. This process was indeed one of the best reasons for shopping at the Emporium.

First, the saleslady wrote out in tiny neat letters a statement of the sale on a little pad lying on the counter.

December 31, 1933
Miss Edith Mullett
One small skein grey worsted @ 8¢
Total 8¢
Amount tendered 10¢

The saleslady placed the bill and Aunt Edith's dime into a little round cartridge and put it into a tube affair behind the counter. She pulled a little bell and—zip!—the cartridge disappeared down the tube to the back of the store where Mr. Cooper himself sat in his office, keeping the store accounts. A minute later the bell rang again and—zip!—the cartridge was back with Aunt Edith's change, two pennies, and the bill now marked "Paid in Full" by Mr. Cooper. There was the same tube affair behind each of the sales counters in the Emporium. Verna had told Margy that her pa claimed this pneumatic tube system was the most up-to-date and efficient way to run a shop, but Aunt Alice privately opined that it was "old Mr. Cooper's way of keeping a tight grip on the reins of the business, especially with scatterbrains like Verna's four sisters behind the counters." Aunt Alice didn't hold with these new-fangled inventions that "sucked money through tubes around the building" so she did most of her shopping at Rainer's, where a real person counted your change into your hand from the cash drawer in front of them. But Margy thought the money tube was terribly modern and exciting, and she never tired of witnessing this strange and interesting contraption at work.

Margy pocketed the change, the receipted bill and the wool, and said, "Thank you, miss," to the saleslady.

Then she started off on her quest.

"Don't forget to visit our ladies' department upstairs," the saleslady called after her as she turned back to her dusting. Saturday morning was rather slow, but the afternoon would bring the crowds of shoppers from the farms around and about the district. It was traditional that all the farm families came into town "to do their trading" and visit up and down the main street every Saturday afternoon. But now the store was almost empty as Margy wandered away.

Ladies' department, she thought disgustedly. Clothes, she thought. I don't want another old pair of kid gloves for Aunt Alice, she thought. *Huh!* she thought. I want something beautiful and useful and practical and . . . well, wonderful.

Just past the Notions department, where Margy had purchased the wool, was the confectionery counter with its array of bright candy in bins and jars: candy kisses, salt water taffy, humbugs, Scotch mints and maple buds, neat packages of chewing gum in two exciting flavours, and "buttons," strips of white paper with sugar tablets stuck along them. Then of course there were George and Snuffy's favourite, thick black licorice "pipes" with sparkly red sugar stuck on the end of the bowl to represent fire. And on the shelf behind the counter, big boxes of chocolates covered with shiny silver paper. Someday, thought Margy dreamily, someday some fellow will bring me a box of chocolates like that and I'll say, kind of careless-like . . . .

What she would say, careless-like, she never decided for at that moment Margy remembered that she was on a Quest. She determinedly turned her back on the confectionery counter.

She wandered through the Emporium in a slow, zigzag pattern. Housewares and dishes, utensils and cutlery, drygoods and blankets, jewellery and ornaments. At the back of the store were the nails and tools, guns and ammunition, saddles and harness and tack, varnish and whitewash, boots and shoes. Nearer the front of the store were all manner of food supplies, from coffee to flour, canned goods to honey. Margy made mental note of a "special" on Proctor and Gamble soap (six bars for twenty-five cents) that she was sure would interest Aunt Edith.

But nothing she saw leapt up and shouted, "I'm the Wonderful Gift for Aunt Alice." Might as well go upstairs and try on some hats, Margy decided, and then this afternoon at home leaf through the Eaton's catalogue. Maybe she could get some ideas there, and Lenore's mother would help her order something and keep it a secret from Aunt Alice. (She couldn't ask Verna's mother for fear of hurting her feelings that there was nothing in the Emporium good enough.)

With no saleswoman in sight, Margy spent a very pleasant fifteen minutes trying on hats in front of the tall mirror by the window. Hats are such fun, she thought, as she settled a wide-brimmed straw "sailor" on her head and looped the long veil over her shoulder. She discarded it—much too summery—for a velvet turban with a rhinestone star pin on the side. She had reluctantly abandoned that as well, and was turning to leave, when she saw it.

The Wonderful Gift for Aunt Alice!

It was just quietly hanging there at the end of a

rack of dresses and coats, but it *was* the Wonderful Gift: a long dressing gown, navy blue wool flannel with matching narrow silk braid around the quilted collar and cuffs. Margy reverently stroked the soft fabric. At the bottom of the sleeve a small tag declared the price to be seven dollars. Such a lot of money, but no sacrifice was too great for Aunt Alice. If Margy started to save right away . . . .

Flushed and triumphant she headed for home. All the way up the hill she considered. Seven dollars. That would be fifty-eight and one-third cents per month for twelve months, or almost two cents a day. That was more than she got in her weekly allowance of ten cents. She would have to think of some way to earn the extra money. But fancy the look on Aunt Alice's face next Christmas morning when she saw the lovely dressing gown.

Margy spent most of the next day after Sunday School was over considering ways to earn money, but none occurred to her. Finally she finished off her homework for the holidays and strapped her books together for the morning. She would think of something. She would find a way.

The next morning Margy wanted to be ready to leave for school early so that she could see all her friends before the bell rang. But by the time she had filled the woodbox and blacked her shoes she had only a minute to get there. She dashed breathlessly into the schoolyard. It was a hubbub of chattering voices.

George sidled up to her as she arrived. "Did you like my gift, Margy?" he asked. She nodded enthusiastically, wishing she knew exactly which animal the woodcarving was supposed to be so she could comment on it more appropriately. "I made it myself," George added, quite unnecessarily.

"It's a beautiful . . . fox," Margy hazarded, coming down on Aunt Alice's side, she being most often right in her pronouncements.

"It weren't a fox, silly. It's a chipmunk. A fox has a much bushier tail." His voice took on the tone of someone explaining a difficult concept to a person who was a little slow. "A chipmunk has a less sharp face than a fox."

Darn, thought Margy. But, "It's an absolutely beautiful chipmunk, George," she said quickly. "I put him on my bedroom window sill and he looks just as natural as can be. I wouldn't be a bit surprised if a real chipmunk came right up to the glass next spring and tried to make friends with him."

"Humph," said George, only somewhat mollified.

But the rest of the day went downhill from there.

The bell rang and the students lined up and filed into the classroom. The first thing Margy noticed as they took off their coats was that Ralph was still wearing his old brown braces. She sat down in her desk pondering this unhappy state of affairs. Didn't he like her scarlet braces?

But this question was quickly driven from her mind, for as Mr. Warren came into the room the whole class could tell that Something was Terribly Wrong.

"Good morning, class," he said in a voice that made it clear the morning was anything but good.

"Good morning, Mr. Warren," answered thirty-two voices in cautious unison.

Opening exercises proceeded through the familiar ritual of singing "O Canada" and the daily Bible reading passage. They stood again and repeated the Lord's Prayer in a droning monotone.

"Please be seated." Mr. Warren stood with his hands behind his back facing the class. They sat down as one and faced him expectantly.

"I have something very sad to tell you," said the teacher. "Sometime over the Christmas holiday our school and classroom were broken into. Only one item was taken." His eyes swept the class. "The only thing that was stolen was the jar containing our donation to the Christmas Cheer Fund. When I went to get the money to give it to Mr. Cooper of the Businessmen's Association, it was gone. *Vanished.* Does anyone know anything about this unfortunate occurrence?"

There was a long pause and a good deal of nervous shuffling and shifting as everyone looked at everyone else. Finally Gwennie put her hand up slowly. Mr. Warren nodded at her.

"My father," she said, her face white, "mentioned yesterday that when he was driving home at dusk on Friday night, he heard some kids fooling around in the schoolyard."

"And?" said Mr. Warren sternly, a question mark in his voice.

"Well, he said that it was a bunch of boys, but he did recognize one girl's voice." Her eyes swung around. "Margy Stratton."

Thirty-one pairs of eyes shifted to Margy who could feel her face turning scarlet.

"But, sir," George was quick to her defence, "A

whole bunch of guys were there, playing shinny . . . and we loaned Margy a hockey stick and she was playing goalie . . . but she had to go in after a while because her aunts said . . . and besides, we all played in the schoolyard over the holiday. . . ." George trailed off. Everybody in the class knew he was kind of sweet on Margy and would defend her no matter what.

"Thank you, George," said Mr. Warren. "You may sit down. Can anyone shed any real light on this?"

There was total and complete silence. Margy wanted to scream, "It wasn't me! Everybody stop looking at me!" But of course she couldn't. Suddenly Verna Cooper gave an involuntary gasp.

"Yes, Verna?" The teacher's voice was dead quiet.

Verna covered her mouth with her hands and shook her head.

"Verna, if you know something, you must tell."

Verna looked miserably at Margy and then at the teacher. "My pa told me, well, that is, he said that Margy spent a long time in the Emporium on Saturday morning looking at things and trying on things . . . and stuff."

Margy stared at Verna in absolute horror. She raged inwardly, Verna, how could you? You're my *friend*. You're in my secret Order of the White Cloud. You're . . . .

But now Orlie Marker at the side of the room had slowly raised his hand.

"Yes?" said Mr. Warren.

"Well, sir," Orlie hesitated and then plunged ahead. "Margy told us once that she wanted to go out west and visit her pa. She'd need lots of money for that."

Margy couldn't believe what she was hearing. She

had said that but it was months ago, one recess when they had all been talking about their fathers for some reason, and someone had said that she didn't have a father. She had bragged that her Daddy owned a big farm out west and she was going to visit him some day. But she didn't think anyone remembered that. And why did it have to be mentioned now, when everyone seemed teamed up against her?

Mr. Warren frowned. It was hard to tell just what he was thinking. There was a long silence as he paced back and forth in front of the blackboard, his hands behind his back. Then he turned and faced the class.

"Marguerite," he said slowly. "I want you to tell me, and I will believe you. Did you or did you not take the money from my desk?"

Margy would have given her soul to be able to stand up smartly and state clearly and emphatically that she had nothing whatsoever to do with the missing money. But her knees had turned to jelly and her voice had turned to fog, and she could only shake her head and stare back at Mr. Warren through tears of frustration and rage.

The teacher studied her further for a moment, and then said briskly, "Well, we'll get nowhere tossing blind accusations around. If anyone knows anything about this situation I want him or her to come to me privately as soon as possible and we'll get this cleared up. In the meantime we'd better just get to work. Senior Fourth, take out your spellers and study the first column of words on page seventy-three; Junior Fourth, you study the words on page sixty-nine of your book."

There was a rustle as the class complied, and a

minute later they were all hunched over their desks, the picture of industry.

All but Margy. She stared at the words unseeing, and when it came time to be tested she got eight of the twenty words wrong.

The morning dragged by on leaden feet. When recess finally came, Margy grabbed her coat off the hook and, without even putting it on, streaked out the door and headed for the safety of the Fine House.

Aunt Alice was in the kitchen when Margy raced through the door. "What are you doing home so early? Did you forget your . . . ."

Margy hurled herself at Aunt Alice and sobbed out the whole story, except of course the reason she had spent so long in the Emporium. "They all think I took the money (sob) . . . I thought they were my friends (sob) . . . I'm never going back there. NEVER! I'll go and live with Daddy."

"But, Margy," said Aunt Alice in a troubled but reasonable voice, "you have to go back or they really will be convinced that you took the money."

"Oh, *please,* Aunt Alice. They all hate me. And I hate them. Don't make me go back."

"Now, Margy, you don't hate anybody. Mr. Warren will sort it out. Like as not he just misplaced the money himself. Or maybe someone who knows the truth has already told him who took it."

But Margy knew the Code of the Schoolyard dictated that no one ever squealed on a friend. And she felt very friendless and alone.

Nevertheless, what Aunt Alice said went. And when the school bell rang for the end of recess, Margy had to stand up straight, stick out her chin and march back to the schoolroom to face the staring eyes of her classmates.

Margy knew she hadn't taken the money. She felt that Mr. Warren knew she hadn't taken the money. Aunt Alice knew she hadn't taken the money. And God in Heaven knew she hadn't taken the money.

But somehow, even with God on her side, Margy felt as if she were in a pathetic minority.

CHAPTER
——3——

For years and years afterwards Margy always thought of the next part of her life as the Lonely Time.

No one came forward to admit to taking the Christmas Cheer money, not even when Constable Parker came to question the class. And Mr. Warren did not discover that he had simply misplaced the money jar.

The gentle Lenore remained constant in her loyalty to Margy, although Margy suspected that this was because the Aunts and Lenore's parents had been life-long friends. As well George was so vocally supportive that some of his friends began to avoid him. And oddly, Orlie Marker, who had never had much to say to Margy before, now got quite chummy. Perhaps, thought Margy, he's trying to make up for telling everyone that I wanted money to go out west to visit Daddy. It was hard not to keep thinking about what he had done to her, but heaven knew she needed all the friends she could get right then.

Most of the rest of the Senior Fourths treated Margy in a cool and mistrustful manner. It was as if she had suddenly gone back to that first day in Room Six almost a year ago, only then the class had viewed her with that mild curiosity and faint disdain reserved for all newcomers. Now it was a deliberate distancing, an arm's-length air of suspicion, that greeted Margy as she came into the classroom. The knot of chattering girls by the coat hooks who suddenly stopped talking and melted away to their desks. The elaborate ritual that Gwennie had of counting all her pencils each morning and announcing with relief to no one particular that they seemed to be all accounted for. The fact that Margy was always picked last for class team activities, and not at all for the games at recess.

Verna Cooper came to Margy with tears in her eyes and said how sorry she was that she had let out the story about Margy's visit to the Emporium. She also said that her Papa had told her she mustn't be friends with Margy any more, and that he said she could not belong to the Order of the White Cloud. There were lots of "regular village girls" that Verna could have for friends, not Margy Stratton. When Verna said that, Margy felt that her "outsider" status was now indelibly carved in stone. And that her heart was broken.

And Ralph. Not that he had ever paid any special attention to her except to play jokes on her or twit her in a good-natured way about her red hair or her glasses. What was Ralph thinking? Did he believe that she could have stolen the money? Why, he and his widowed mother were likely one of the very families that might have benefited from the Christmas Cheer Fund. Margy felt a wide gulf between them, much wider than from her seat at the front of the room to his at the back.

He didn't call her "Four-Eyes" any more, or put

broken chalk inside her inkwell. And what made it worse was that Gwennie seemed always to be at Ralph's elbow, smiling and simpering, cajoling and manoeuvring into his circle. Why, it was all over the classroom that Gwennie had drawn Ralph's name at Christmas and had given him a hitherto undisclosed but expensive and intimate gift. And it was true that Ralph and Gwennie sometimes left the schoolyard together heading for the skating rink.

Margy left the school grounds the minute that class was over. She kept to herself, and tried not to think about the round of wintertime activities she was missing out on. But it was impossible not to think about something that was always there—like a bad smell, or a gloomy cloud, or a high invisible wall separating her from everyone else. In truth she spent most of her time thinking about it, wondering what did happen to the Christmas Cheer money jar, who might have taken it, and when and how and why, and whether the Truth would ever be known, or if she would simply spend the rest of her life under the cloud of suspicion, and wondering, wondering . . . .

If only she hadn't gone out to play hockey with the fellows that evening . . . if only she hadn't said something just at the exact moment when Gwennie's father drove past . . . if only she hadn't bragged to Orlie about visiting her Daddy's farm. . . . Margy's emotions ranged from regret and despair to anger and downright defiance, but of course all these feelings were kept carefully inside her. On the outside she tried to act as if nothing had happened, and held her head up high as she walked through life all by herself.

Aunt Alice was, as usual, the mainstay of Margy's life during the Lonely Time. She kept saying, "Who cares what the outside world thinks, as long as you know you're innocent?" But Margy knew that both Aunts *did* care what the village thought; they were simply trying to rise above it. Aunt Alice had even more reason not to go into Cooper's Emporium now. And even in Rainer's Hardware, where the Mulletts had dealt ever since Grandfather advanced Mr. Rainer the money to get started, there was an uncomfortable undercurrent. It had taken less than twenty-four hours for the story of the missing Christmas Cheer money to get around the village.

As the weeks went by, Margy went out less and less, a prisoner within the walls of distrust that had been built up around her. Both Aunt Alice and Aunt Edith seemed to feel that time and the Truth would exonerate Margy. In the meantime they threw their energies into finding distractions that would compensate for Margy's lack of social activities.

Aunt Alice promised a Special Present that would arrive in a week or so. Margy suspected it was probably something that Aunt Edith was knitting and had not quite finished, or perhaps a book that Aunt Alice had ordered for her through the library. But when Margy tried to guess, Aunt Alice just smiled mysteriously and said nothing.

For the time being both Aunts urged that Margy take advantage of this lull in her life to concentrate on her schoolwork, since they both hoped that she would do well in the Entrance Examinations and go on to the Continuation School in the fall. She would be the first in the family to go to high school and Aunt Alice had great expectations for Margy's success. Both Aunts drilled Margy mercilessly on her spelling, so much so that she got a perfect score in the Friday tests three weeks running.

They also pointed out that now would be a good time to "get cracking on that Memory Work." (Margy had earlier made the mistake of mentioning that she was required to learn two hundred lines of poetry by the end of the school year to get a pass in English Literature.)

"Yes, indeed," said Aunt Alice enthusiastically. "Did the teacher assign what you had to memorize, Margy?"

"No," (dolefully), "Mr. Warren just said that it had to be written by a Canadian poet."

"Marvellous! There are some *wonderful* Canadian poets." Aunt Alice ticked them off on her fingers. "Archibald Lampman, Pauline Johnston, Charles C.D. Roberts, Charles Sangster . . . ."

"And Lilian Leveridge, Alice. Don't forget Lilian Leveridge." Aunt Edith turned proudly to Margy. "She's a famous poetess who lives just south of here in Wollaston Township. Beautiful poetry, dear. You *must* learn some of hers."

Aunt Edith struck an elocutionary stance and recited "Over the Hills of Home," written by Miss Leveridge for her beloved brother who had been killed overseas in the Great War. It was a beautiful poem, but oh, so sad.

After a respectable silence Margy said, "That was very nice, Auntedith, but I really don't see the point of memorizing things. If I want to read a poem I can just get a book and look it up."

"The *point?*" Aunt Alice stared at Margy as if she had said something blasphemous. "The *point* is to train your memory so that it will then be able to retain other valuable and important information you want to store in it."

"Yes," Aunt Edith chimed in, "What if you're a guest at a grand house party and everyone else gets up and does their 'Party Piece' for the entertainment, sings a song or does some magic tricks, and there you are without even a recitation to do. A proper dummy you'd feel, wouldn't you?"

Margy glowered in the face of this enthusiasm. As if, she thought, as if I'll ever get invited to a "grand house party." I'm not even going to the skating party at the village rink tonight.

"Or," (Aunt Edith was warming to her subject), "suppose you go to help out when there's a death in a family, and you want to whip up a pan of biscuits or a wacky cake. You have to know the ingredients and the quantities or you'd be in the embarrassing position of having to borrow a recipe book." Margy could tell by the Aunt's scandalized tone that she was never in that embarrassing position.

"Exactly," said Aunt Alice. "Or you need to recall addresses, or birthdays, or your bank pass book number. You have to *train* your memory ahead of time. In its natural state the human brain is like a sieve. Now then, I'll bring some poetry books home from the library on Tuesday and you can select something you'd like to learn. You're a quick study. It will be just like learning the lines for that play you were in last fall."

Margy groaned inwardly. Learning lines for the play had been fun. This promised to be just plain hard work. *Two hundred lines.* Perhaps she would be able to find something in one of Aunt Alice's library books that had little tiny short lines.

"In the meantime," Aunt Alice continued, "I saved the crossword puzzle out of this week's *Bancroft Times* for you to do. Excellent training for memory and spelling. You can get it done by bedtime if you start right now."

"Yes, Auntalice." Margy sighed. She got a pencil and sharpened it into the woodstove with the kitchen paring knife. Then she sat glumly at the kitchen table. Aunt Edith settled down to some socks that needed darning. Aunt Alice said that her eyes were too tired to mend so she rocked in Grandfather's old rocking chair by the woodstove.

Crossword puzzles were a brand-new phenomenon sweeping the country and recently picked up by the local paper. They had to do with fitting intersecting words into a small grid with some of the spaces blacked out. It was all very complicated. Margy thought, how can crossword puzzles help my spelling when I can't spell the words in the first place? She opened the paper to the back page and licked the pencil lead.

"First clue, 'one across,'" said Aunt Alice.

"A word with," (Margy counted), "seven letters meaning 'precisely,'" she read dutifully.

"'Exactly,'" shot in Aunt Edith smugly. "Write it in."

"Really, Edith," said Aunt Alice, "You could let the girl figure it out on her own."

Margy printed the word into the grid. "Doesn't fit," she said.

Aunt Alice's eyebrows went up. "Spell it out."

Margy sighed. "E-G-G-Z . . ."

"Not 'egg-zactly,' Margy. 'EX-actly.' How can you possibly hope to spell it correctly if you don't pronounce it properly?"

"Yes, Auntalice." Margy licked her finger and tried to rub out the offending word. Her finger went right through the paper. She had to print extra hard to make the new letters show up. She wrote E-X-A-C-T-L-E-Y. It still didn't fit.

Now it was Aunt Edith's turn to sigh. "There is no 'E' before the 'Y.'" At this rate it would take until midnight to complete the crossword puzzle. "Try 'one down,' dear. We know it will begin with an 'E.' How many letters?"

Margy intended to read the next clue but an advertisement beside the puzzle caught her eye. It read:

Earn $35 weekly at home
growing Mushrooms for us all year round.
We start you and contract to buy
all you grow at top prices.
Full particulars for 10¢.
IDEAL MUSHROOM COMPANY, Islington.

Margy's eyes lit up. Thirty-five dollars a week! If she and the Aunts grew mushrooms in the cellar of the Fine House, why, they could be rich in no time.

And just wait until she was rich, richer even than Gwennie. Then just see how much she cared about what anyone else in the village thought. Then they would be sorry they had treated her so badly. Why, they'd be lining up to be friends with her again. But with her very first week's profit, Margy would buy Aunt Alice's Wonderful Gift, and maybe one for Aunt Edith too. They were the only people who really understood Margy and had never stopped believing in her. Yes, with her very first mushroom crop she would show the Aunts how much she appreciated them.

"The clue for 'one down,' Margy?" Aunt Alice interrupted her reverie.

"Listen to this, Auntalice!" Margy excitedly read them the advertisement. She was a little surprised none of them had noticed it before. "We'd be *rich!*"

Aunt Edith and Aunt Alice exchanged a long look. Then Aunt Alice looked at Margy for a long time before she answered.

"Margy dear," she said gently, "The only one who gets rich from that kind of scheme is the person who put the advertisement in the paper in the first place. He gets ten cents from every person who is lazy and greedy enough to believe him. And even more money from the people who agree to buy all the equipment from him. I expect that he's the only one who makes thirty-five dollars a week."

"But, Auntalice . . ."

"Margy," Aunt Alice's voice was even gentler, "Why do you want money so much? Don't you have everything you need here? Don't you like living with us?"

Margy nodded her head slowly, unwilling to give up on the mushroom idea so quickly, unwilling to explain why she needed the money.

Aunt Alice rocked back and forth in Grandfather's

old chair for a long time. Finally she said, "Put the newspaper away, Margy. I'm going to tell you a story, one my father told me a long time ago. Then I want you to go to bed and think about it."

Margy obediently folded the newspaper in her lap and turned to Aunt Alice expectantly. This is Aunt Alice's story:

"There were once two brothers who were accused of stealing sheep from their neighbour's farm. The two brothers did not take the sheep, but everyone in the village believed that they had done so, and at the trial they were declared guilty. They were both sentenced to a year in jail. Not only that, but they each had the letters ST branded on their cheek to warn everyone forever that they were convicted sheep thieves.

"After the year was over they were released from jail. The older brother packed his few belongings, left the village and wandered from place to place, carrying the brand of his shame. He died alone and bitter in a foreign land, where he was buried, unmarked and unmourned, in a forgotten grave.

"But when the younger brother was released from prison, he went back to his little farm on the edge of the village and began to scrape and toil and labour. By the sweat of his brow and by years of unblinking honesty he finally won back the respect and affection of his fellow townspeople, and eventually became burgomaster of the community.

"Years later a visitor to the village asked a little boy what the letters ST branded into the mayor's cheek meant. The lad, who had never been told the real story, thought about it for a minute and then said to the visitor, 'I'm not sure, but I think those letters stand for saint.'"

Aunt Alice finished her story and gave Margy another long hard look. "Now, off you go to bed," she said. "Goodnight, dear. Don't forget to say your prayers."

Margy said goodnight to the Aunts and headed off up the stairs. She knew that Aunt Alice thought she could simply live down the unfair shadow over her name, but Aunt Alice didn't have people stop talking when she came into a room, or worse yet, whisper behind their hands. She knew that the Aunts thought she wanted money to run away from Bancroft and go to live with Daddy out west, but how could she tell them about the Wonderful Gift and ruin the surprise. After she said her prayers Margy lay in the dark for a long time, feeling as if she were drowning in the murky waters of misunderstanding with no solid rock to cling to.

The following week Aunt Alice brought home a pile of poetry books. On Saturday after chores she laid them in an inviting array on the kitchen table. Margy listlessly thumbed through them as she ate her afternoon snack and thought about the movie she wasn't at just then. Some of the poetry didn't even rhyme. And the lines were way too long. Pretty boring stuff, she thought. Impossible to memorize.

Aunt Edith looked up from the counter where she was stirring up some biscuits for supper. "There's a small book with some Lilian Leveridge poetry upstairs in your Grandfather's old room," she said hopefully. "Why don't you take a look at that?"

Margy dutifully dragged herself to her feet and

headed up the stairs. She found the slim book on the bottom shelf wedged in with other dusty volumes and pulled it out with difficulty. Stamped on the front cover was the title *Canadian Singers and Their Songs.*

The book cracked slightly as she opened it. Each page featured a photograph of the poet and one of his or her poems reproduced in the poet's own handwriting. Some of the pages were really quite difficult to read because the writing was so ornate or cramped, or both.

Margy ran her eye across the first poem: "Alone," by Hilda Maude Florence Huskinson Starr.

Alone, alone, alone, without a friend to care;
Alone, alone, alone, with all my grief to bear . . .

Margy sighed. Hilda Maude Florence seemed to be in much the same boat as she was. The only difference was that Hilda Maude Florence had written a depressing long poem about it in order to wallow in her misery. Margy flipped over to find the Leveridge piece. Yes, that would be it: "Over the Hills of Home."

She was about to head back downstairs. But before she stood up she let her eye run across the other books in the bottom shelf. A thick, dilapidated volume with a dark cover and an indecipherable title caught her attention. She pulled the book out and flipped it open.

More poetry. Her eye fell on a verse:

A bunch of the boys were whooping it up
    in the Malamute Saloon;

The kid that handles the music-box
                    was hitting a jag-time tune;
Back of the bar, in a solo game,
                    sat Dangerous Dan McGrew . . .

Now, here was *poetry!*

Margy scanned the Table of Contents. "The Ballad of Blasphemous Bill," "The Ballad of One-Eyed Mike," "The Ballad of Pious Pete." Immediately following the index there was brief biography of Mr. Service which Margy also scanned. It said that the poet had been born in England but had moved to Canada in his early twenties, and that the poems were written while he lived in Vancouver working in a bank. Margy decided that if a poem were written on Canadian soil it should be deemed "Canadian poetry," even if the poet had been born in darkest Africa.

She also knew that a poem that contained the line, "One of you is a hound of hell/And that one is Dan McGrew," would not be considered entirely suitable by Aunt Alice as a "Party Piece." Still, if the book were on Grandfather's shelf it must be all right. Margy carried the battered volume into her bedroom and slipped it under the mattress beside the *Bancroft Times* with the mushroom advertisement.

Then she took the slim volume called *Canadian Singers and Their Songs* downstairs, propped it up on the kitchen table, helped herself to another apple, and started to memorize "Over the Hills." Aunt Edith smiled approvingly.

After supper Margy listened to "Amos 'n Andy" on the radio in the parlour and tried not to think of the other Senior Fourths enjoying the Saturday evening of winter fun. She had heard the boys planning a grand hockey match for the skating rink this weekend. The Turks, all boys from that part of the village known as Turkey Flats, would go up against the Cowbells, the team from Cow Bell Alley. The winners of that game would play the Pideys on Saturday right after supper. The Pideys were the team from "Piety Hill," that neighbourhood inhabited in their fine houses by the "doctors, lawyers, and merchant chiefs" of Bancroft. Their team boasted real hockey sweaters, real pucks and, best of all, honest-to-goodness hockey pads. The Cowbells made do with old Eaton's Catalogues stuffed down their pant legs, and the hardy Turks went without pads at all.

And then after the hockey match was over, the girls who had been tobogganing on the Cleak Street Hill would come to warm themselves at the bonfire by the rink, and someone would no doubt produce some hot dogs to cook, or suggest going to her house for cocoa, and they would play Snap until all hours and go straggling home at nine-thirty or ten. . . . But of course she wouldn't be there at all so it didn't matter, did it?

Margy had heard all the whispered arrangements at recess the day before. She knew that everyone was invited to Verna's house after the sliding. She had heard Gwennie announce that she would bring some homemade maple walnut fudge.

And when Margy had asked Lenore after school if she wanted to come over on Saturday night after supper to play Parcheesi with her, Lenore had just looked stricken and said she had been invited to Verna's.

"But I don't have to go, Margy. I can come to your house instead. I'd be *glad* to do that."

Margy heard herself reply in a slightly lofty tone, "No, Lenore, you go along with the rest. Actually I might have other plans for Saturday night anyway."

Lenore had looked torn between doubt and relief, but they parted at the gate at that point and the conversation had ended. Now Margy wished her pride hadn't got the better of her and Lenore was there right now.

Instead Margy sat in the parlour with her Aunts listening to Amos 'n Andy and the Kingfisher and Sapphire on the radio, trying to laugh at their silly adventures and feeling bluer and bluer by the moment. It was all so unfair.

As the program ended there was a sharp rap at the back door. Aunt Alice rose stiffly and said, "I'll get that. You two stay here." She shot Aunt Edith a significant look and then disappeared into the hall towards the kitchen.

Margy looked at Aunt Edith who had suddenly become very occupied fiddling with the dials on the radio, trying to tune in the Jack Benny Showcase. Finally the announcer's voice emerged through the waves of static. "Mr. Benny's special guest for this evening is Mr. Bing Crosby, who has crooned his way into a million hearts since his movie debut three years ago. His dulcet voice will make you want to sing right along."

But Margy wasn't paying attention to the announcer's enthusiastic words. She was much more interested in the sounds from the back of the house: the murmur of voices, the opening and closing of the back door several times, the odd "scrabbly" sound.

Aunt Alice's head popped around the door frame of the parlour and she said, with a self-satisfied smile, "Margy dear, would you come out to the kitchen? There's someone here who would like to meet you."

Margy stood up slowly and started for the door with dragging feet. Surely Aunt Alice wouldn't have gone off and lined up somebody to be her "friend." That would be the most humiliating thing of all, but she wouldn't put it past her Aunt.

They stepped into the kitchen. There's no one here, thought Margy.

Then she saw him, sitting on the floor by the back door. He had long droopy ears and the saddest eyes she'd ever seen staring out of his brown fur face. A big old ugly lop-eared hound dog!

Margy clapped her hands over her mouth and whispered, "Oh, Auntalice . . . OH, Auntalice . . . He's . . . ," (she searched for a word), "He's *beautiful!*" She knelt carefully in front of the dog and slowly extended her hand so he could sniff it. "Is he ours?"

"He's yours, Margy," said Aunt Alice. "Do you like him?"

Margy could do nothing but whisper again, "He's beautiful."

Aunt Edith laughed. " 'Beauty is certainly in the eye of the beholder' then."

"But where did he come from?" By now Margy had her hand on the neck of the dog, stroking his sleek fur. The dog responded with a cautious wag of his tail.

"Mr. Black from out on the Winter Road came into

the library the other day," explained Aunt Alice. "Said that he had a young coon hound to get rid of, no good as a 'cooner' at all, and if I heard of anyone wanting a pet to let him know. The more I thought about it, the more it sounded like a good idea to have a dog around the place." She looked mightily pleased at the success of her surprise. "I asked Mr. Black to drop him off tonight when he came into town to shop. The way Mr. Black described him I thought he would be a little more elegant looking."

"What's his name?" By now Margy had both hands on the dog and was scratching him behind his floppy ears. The dog licked her face with his long rough tongue.

"Name?" said Aunt Alice. "I don't think the poor animal has a name. Mr. Black just called him 'Hound.' I guess you'll have to name him yourself, Margy."

"You could give him a traditional name," said Aunt Edith helpfully, "like 'Toby' or 'Rex.' Or a classical name like 'Caesar' or 'Cerberus.'"

"Do any of those appeal to you, Margy?" asked Aunt Alice. "I could look some others up when I go to the library on Monday."

Margy put her arms around the dog's neck and buried her face in his soft sweet-smelling fur. His tail thumped companionably on the kitchen floor. She hesitated. Naming her dog wasn't something she wanted to do on the spur of the moment. No indeed, something as important as this might take some time. The name couldn't be too common; it had to reflect something special about the animal, his personality or his talents. Maybe it would be "Fido" to show that he was her faithful friend, or "Buddy" or "Pal" to indicate that he was her special companion. "I'll have to *consider* a name, Auntalice," said Margy firmly.

"That's fine, Margy," said Aunt Alice, becoming practical and businesslike. "That dog will be your responsibility. You'll have to feed him and walk him and look after him."

Margy nodded happily. It seemed as if the hound nodded too.

"And he must *not* go upstairs at all. And not in the dining room when we're eating."

"Yes, Auntalice."

"Now let's go back and listen to Jack Benny and then you can take your new dog for a walk before you go to bed."

Margy unhooked the bindertwine leash from the kitchen doorknob and the hound trotted quite contentedly beside her into the parlour. He plopped down beside Aunt Alice's feet and Margy sat on the rug beside him so she could stroke his back. He certainly seemed a quiet, well-behaved animal for an erstwhile hunting hound.

That is, he seemed quiet and well-behaved until Jack Benny brought on his special guest, and Bing Crosby began to sing "Where the Blue of the Night Meets the Gold of the Day." Buddy immediately sat up, threw back his angular head, and began to sing along, with long mournful howls that rose and fell with the music.

The Aunts and Margy laughed until tears were running down their faces.

"Not a 'cooner,' but definitely a 'crooner,'" said Aunt

Alice when she recovered the power of speech, and that set them all off again. As soon as the song ended, the dog settled back into his relaxed position on the carpet and turned his sad banjo eyes to Margy in mute request that she resume her stroking.

When the Jack Benny Showcase was over, Aunt Alice dug out her purse and gave Margy a dollar bill. "You take your friend 'Bing Crosby' here," (and no one ever called him anything but "Bing" ever after), "for a walk, and stop at Rainer's Hardware to buy him a big bag of dog biscuits. You can use them for rewards to train your new dog to obey you. I meant to pick up some when I went down street, but I was just feeling so poorly that I came straight home from the library today." It was strange to hear the stoical Aunt Alice comment on her health. Aunt Edith shot her a concerned look, but Aunt Alice said briskly, "Now, off you go, Margy. Keep 'Bing' on his rope for a few days until he knows he belongs to you."

Margy stepped out into the raw January wind, her dog trotting happily by her side. Before I get the biscuits, she thought, I'll just wander nonchalantly past the tobogganing hill and skating rink to let them all see that I've got better things to do, like walk my new dog. When Lenore sees me she'll probably rush over and all the rest will just trail along too. Maybe they'll ask me if I want to slide, and they'll fight over who gets to hold my dog's rope while I have a go down the hill. The more she thought about this, the more reasonable the possibility sounded to Margy, and she turned her feet towards the Cleak Street hill.

As she approached the slope she could make out a

cluster of girls at the top in the crisp moonlight. They were laughing, and trying to cram together onto Gwennie's large toboggan. Lenore, the smallest in stature, was jammed at the front, and behind her Verna Cooper, with Cora Parker kneeling at the back. Seconds later they were off down the hill towards Margy, a blur among the other sliders. They ended in a laughing heap at the bottom as Margy stood in the shadow of the great gnarled tree that leaned over the road at the foot of the hill.

The three girls untangled themselves and immediately turned to climb the hill again, Verna instructing Lenore on how to steer better, and Lenore not paying the slightest attention but trying to wash Cora's face with a mittenful of snow. Bing looked up at Margy encouragingly, as if to say let's join the fun, but Margy pulled on his rope and together they melted backwards into the deeper shadows of the tree.

She watched a moment longer, feeling as if she were seeing the hillside scene as an illustration in a novel or on the front of a Christmas card, so far removed was she from the others and their fun. She turned and slipped away towards Hastings Street, as silent as the wintry moonlight. Avoiding the skating rink at the corner, she went straight up the main street to Rainer's Hardware Store. Bing, the picture of obedient companionship, trotted happily at her side.

She tied Bing securely to the post outside Rainer's Store and entered the shop. It was bustling and noisy with the Saturday night crowd. She walked right past the small but enticing candy counter to the bulk feed counter directly beyond it.

Mr. Rainer himself served her. Margy had liked Mr. Rainer ever since she came to Bancroft, even before he had given her the bargain on the scarlet suspenders. He didn't have any children of his own but he was kind to all the kids who came in with their pennies for treats, even when they spent ten minutes figuring out how best to spend a nickel. Sometimes he even gave a free licorice whip to a small child who didn't have any money to spend. Moreover, he hadn't made Margy feel like an outcast in the weeks since Christmas. In the few times she had come to run errands for the Aunts, Margy always hoped that Mr. Rainer would be the one to serve her in the store.

Mr. Rainer weighed out the dog biscuits in the candy scale, bagged them, and dug into the cash register for Margy's change.

"Not at the hockey match, Margy?" he asked. "Your friends came through here a while ago, stocking up on candy for the skating rink."

My friends, thought Margy. My friends, *huh!* But she said aloud, "I don't have time to go to the rink. I've got to train my new dog."

"A new dog, eh? Ain't that nice." Mr. Rainer counted the three quarters change into her hand. "Twenty-five cents for the biscuits, that's fifty, seventy-five and one dollar."

Margy stood mesmerized, staring at the coins in her hand.

Mr. Rainer smiled at her. "Ain't that right, lass?"

With shaking fingers Margy held up one of the coins, a very shiny American quarter minted in 1919. Her voice came from somewhere very far away, like the bottom of her boots. "Do you know where you got this coin, Mr. Rainer?"

The shopkeeper looked over his glasses at it and smiled. "It's all right, lass; it's legal tender. One of your friends just spent it here a while ago, on his way to the hockey match."

"Do you remember who, Mr. Rainer? It's very important." Margy's voice was a whisper.

"Well now, as a matter of fact, I do that," said Mr. Rainer easily. "I especially remarked on it to myself because it was a young chap who comes in all the time but almost never has any money to spend. But he's been in several times since Christmas and tonight he was buying treats for everybody with a big handful of change. Said his aunt sent it to him from Sudbury for Christmas."

"His name, Mr. Rainer. Do you know his name?" Margy spoke urgently. A swarm of customers was coming up behind her and already Mr. Rainer was turning away towards them.

"His name's Orlie, I think. Big family. Live out on the Mud Road."

Margy picked up the bag of dog cookies and walked unseeing to the door. She untied her dog and turned mechanically towards home. All the way she explained the situation to Bing. He loped alongside her, listening and plainly trying to understand.

"And so, Bing, I still don't know what to do. If I squeal on Orlie I might clear my own name but the other kids, especially Orlie's friends, will be mad at me for ratting. And what if it isn't the same quarter? What if his aunt did send him a lot of money for Christmas?"

Bing muzzled his furry nose into her mittened hand in an understanding way.

Margy stopped and dug a dog biscuit out of the paper bag. She gave it to Bing who crunched it eagerly. "Yes," she said to him, as if he had made a good suggestion, "I shall discuss it with Aunt Alice when we get home. She'll know what I should do. She always knows what to do."

But when Margy got home Aunt Alice had already gone to bed with a sick headache. Margy found an old soft blanket and made Bing a nice bed on the floor beside the woodstove in the kitchen.

"Goodnight, Bing," she whispered. "Tomorrow morning after we get home from church we'll talk to Auntalice." And she thought, I'll thank her properly for my beautiful doggy friend. Margy kissed Bing on the end of his wet black nose.

But Margy was not able to talk to Aunt Alice the next morning, or for many weeks after.

CHAPTER
——4——

The house was quiet. Too quiet. Even the gusty wind of February that buffeted the Fine House from outside seemed muffled and far away.

Margy stayed in her room reading *A Tangled Web* over and over, or if she ventured out, tiptoed downstairs in her stockinged feet. Conversations were short and conducted in an urgent whisper. Yes, the house was too quiet indeed.

The only sound was Aunt Alice's rasping and shallow breathing. It seemed to resound from her bedroom throughout the entire house. As Margy lay on her bed trying to read, the harsh sound penetrated the wall beside her.

Pneumonia, Dr. Landy had said. And he had been seen to shake his head several times over the past few weeks. He had quickly arranged for a real nurse to stay right there in the Fine House to look after Aunt Alice. Certainly Aunt Edith was not much use in a crisis, and with her wobbly legs she couldn't manage going up and down stairs a lot.

Margy wanted to help out but she didn't know what to do. The best she could manage was to stay out of sight and keep quiet, and just go through the motions of school and living. But it was so sad and lonely without Aunt Alice to talk to. It seemed like forever since that evening so many weeks ago, that wonderful evening when Margy got Bing, that terrible evening when she had discovered that Orlie Marker had spent her special quarter at Mr. Rainer's store. And the next morning, just when Margy needed to talk to Aunt Alice, she hadn't come down to breakfast because she was getting such a dreadful cold, which just kept getting worse and worse until Dr. Landy said that awful word, pneumonia.

Margy knew that the crisis was at hand, that time when Aunt Alice would either give up the struggle and join Momma in the Beautiful Land, or turn the corner towards recovery. Margy knew this time had come by the way Aunt Edith and the trained nurse would stop talking abruptly when she came into the room. And by the fact that Dr. Landy dropped in twice or three times a day, and came late at night, and shook his head as he was leaving Aunt Alice's bedroom.

And so Margy lay in her own bedroom. Supper was over, her homework was done, dark had snugged in around the Fine House, and there was nothing to do but wait for the Change to come. Aunt Edith had told her to go to sleep and perhaps by morning they would know, one way or the other. But sleep did not come and so Margy, as usual, turned to an old friend, a book.

She read the same paragraph three times and still had not the slightest idea of what it said.

The nurse padded past her door on rubber soles, heading for Aunt Alice's room. A moment later the door of Margy's bedroom nudged open a few inches and Bing slipped silently through the crack. Margy invited him up onto the bed and pulled the quilt around them and up over their heads. Anything to block out the sound of Aunt Alice's tortured breathing.

Under the heavy quilt it was dark and warm and quiet. But even in the cosy space where she and Bing curled together there was lots of room to think big thoughts, thoughts about Aunt Alice and life and death.

Death. It could be so quick and sudden. Aunt Alice said that death was just another part of life, and the greatest adventure of all, the doorway to the Beautiful Place. She said that we mustn't feel sorry for people who died, but be happy for them, because death wasn't the end of their lives, just the end of their troubles.

Margy felt more sorry for the people who were left behind, because maybe their troubles were just beginning. After all, what would happen to her if anything happened to Aunt Alice? Margy knew this was a selfish way to look at it, but she knew how quickly and drastically a person's life could change through no fault of her own.

Why, just the week before Amy Lawson's mother had died. Mrs. Lawson was going to have another baby, but the baby came too soon and died in his mother's arms—and then she died a few hours later. And now Amy had to leave Senior Fourth because her father needed her at home to look after her little brothers and sisters. Amy, who was as smart as a whip and planned to go on to Continuation School and be a school teacher some day. Death had a terrible way of turning everyone's life upside down.

In the quiet and the dark Margy forced herself to think back, five long years ago, to the sad time when her Momma had left her, just like Amy's. Momma had been sick for such a long time, for years, and finally Aunt Edith had come out west to Daddy's farm to fetch her back home to Grandfather's Fine House for a last visit. Here she had died, in the same room, in the same bed, where Aunt Alice now lay.

Everyone said it was a blessing when Momma died. Margy could never understand this. To her it would have been a blessing if Momma had not got sick in the first place. Why would it be a blessing for God to let Momma suffer so and then take her away?

Margy closed her eyes and felt a tear soak into the pillow. A kaleidoscope of images danced before her eyes: beautiful, graceful Momma with her soft hair piled on the back of her head and her blue-grey eyes dancing with fun; then Momma growing thinner and weaker and quieter; and finally the long hot train ride back east with Aunt Edith the summer Momma died.

But mostly Margy remembered her last long talk with Momma. That was what she missed most of all— those delicious long talks when she had Momma all to herself. That last talk was a special memory that Margy had played over and over in her mind many times.

It had been only a few days before Momma died. Aunt Edith and Aunt Alice were in the kitchen and Grandfather was down street on business. Eight-year-old Margy was tiptoeing past the door of the blue bedroom where Momma lay in the wide white bed. She heard Momma's gentle voice call her name.

Momma told her to shut the door and then invited her to climb up on the bed and snuggle in beside her. They talked a bit but Momma was very weak so mostly they just lay beside one another, Margy in the crook of Momma's arm.

Finally Momma's soft voice had said, "Margy, are you awake?"

Margy nodded.

"Margy, my love, you know that soon I'm going to the Better Land where there is no pain."

Margy hugged Momma harder and tighter.

"Except for missing you and your Daddy, your Aunts and Grandfather, I don't even mind." Her voice broke. "It's just that I'm *so* tired.

Margy swallowed a sob and nodded.

"But Margy sweet, if you ever need me I'll be right there beside you. You don't even need to call my name because I'll be there already." Momma's voice was so quiet now that Margy had to listen with all her strength. She went on, "It says in the Bible that everybody has a guardian angel, and I'm going to ask your angel if I can help keep a watch over you. That way you won't ever have to be afraid because we'll be there together with you."

Momma was tired out by this long talk and soon drifted off to sleep. Margy didn't want to wake her by moving so she just stayed there, curled up in Momma's arm until she fell asleep herself. That was where Grandfather found them when he came in an hour later.

And in three more days it was all over. Momma had quietly "put her hand into the hand of God and stepped off into Eternity." That was what Grandfather said.

Margy's thoughts lingered on her Grandfather. He looked so stern and dignified in his black suit and full white beard. Most people didn't know what a kind and gentle person he was underneath. But Margy knew. And so her memories of the day of Momma's death always ended with him.

The day after the funeral Margy and Daddy, who had come from the west just before Momma died, left for home and Margy never saw her Grandfather again. Her very last memory of him was saying goodbye at the train station. Grandfather had pressed into her hand two whole dimes to spend on treats on the trip west. Margy had spent those dimes long ago, but the silver half-dollar her Grandfather had sent for her birthday the following year had become one of her most valued possessions. She had never even considered spending it, not even for Aunt Alice's Wonderful Gift.

Margy's thoughts returned to the present. Momma was gone. Grandfather was gone. And now Aunt Alice . . . .

Bing awoke and burrowed closer to Margy. She draped her arm over his warm furry body under the quilt.

"It's only, Bing," she whispered, "It's only that everybody I just get to depend on always leaves me."

Bing sighed and pushed his nose against her wet cheek.

"Yes," replied Margy, "There is Auntedith. But somehow she just isn't . . . ." She struggled for the right word to explain it to Bing. She wanted to say, "Auntedith just isn't Auntalice," but that would be no help to him, so instead she said, "Auntedith just isn't *dependable*."

It was true. Aunt Alice was a solid oak tree that a hurricane could not uproot; Aunt Edith was a slender reed that pitched and tossed in the slightest breeze. Aunt Alice rose to her utmost strength in a crisis; Aunt Edith collapsed in dithery confusion at the slightest upset. Why, just yesterday Aunt Edith had burst into tears when she discovered her pet geranium all wilted in its pot on the kitchen window sill. And the day before she had nearly had a conniption when the hired nurse accidentally broke the handle off an old teacup.

"Of course," Margy whispered to Bing, "To be fair it might have just been that Auntedith was already so upset about Auntalice."

Yes, Aunt Edith must also be wondering about what she would do if anything happened to her sister, with no one to earn a small salary at the library, and no one to organize the household, paying the bills and remembering to order the wood for the winter. What would any of them do without Aunt Alice?

And once again, Margy would have no one to have long talks with. She would miss that most of all if anything happened to Aunt Alice. Aunt Alice, who was smart and practical, but who didn't give advice until she was asked. And who listened as much as she talked when they were discussing important matters, like whether Mrs. Montgomery would write another book soon, or if a person read every single book in the world, would she know *everything*. You could never discuss these important matters with Aunt Edith.

A sudden flash of realization came to Margy there in the dark under the quilt—so sudden that she jumped and even Bing woke up again. Margy realized that one of the reasons she loved Aunt Alice more than Aunt Edith was because Aunt Alice was not only smart and practical, she was independent too. And Margy wanted to be just like her. Smart and practical and most of all independent, so that she wouldn't have to lean on anyone else in the world for advice or help or comfort.

"Be just like Auntalice," she whispered in Bing's ear. "She doesn't take anything from anybody. She makes her own decisions and sticks to 'em, and doesn't back off from any problem, just marches right up to it and spits in its eye." The question was, could Aunt Alice spit in the eye of death?

Margy vowed, right then and there in the dark under Momma's crazy quilt with Bing as a witness, that whatever happened to Aunt Alice, whether she lived or died, she, Marguerite Stratton, would strive every day to be more and more like Aunt Alice, independent and fearless. And that she would confront Orlie Marker with her suspicions, *make* him confess that he had taken the money, and clear her own name of the shadow over it.

"Yes, I will," she said right out loud in the darkness. She could feel Bing's rope tail thump against her leg under the cover as if in agreement.

Having made this resolution, Margy suddenly found herself overcome with a profound peace and tiredness. The exhaustion of "wrestling with an angel," Aunt Alice would have said. She pulled Bing's soft limp form closer in her arms and closed her eyes.

The next thing she was aware of was a presence in her room, standing over her and gently shaking her awake.

Margy emerged from under the quilt. The room

was dark and Aunt Edith stood over her, silhouetted by the dim light from the hall.

"What . . ." Margy started, then stopped in horror. The silence of the house overwhelmed her. There was no sound at all of Aunt Alice's laboured breathing.

Margy clutched at Aunt Edith. "Auntalice . . . ?" was all she could muster.

Aunt Edith enveloped her in a large hug. "It's all right, Margy. It's all right. The fever has finally broken and she's resting natural now. The nurse is sure she's turned the corner."

They clung to each other in the darkness. Margy had never felt closer to Aunt Edith.

Finally her Aunt said, this time her voice sharp with relief, "She's awake and asking for you. Run quick and wash your face and run a comb through your hair. You look like the 'Wreck of the Hesperus.' And for heaven's sake, send that wretched animal back downstairs where he belongs."

Margy was up in a flash. The nurse met them outside Aunt Alice's door a minute later. She whispered to Margy in a starchy sort of voice, "Just stay for a moment, Margy. She's very weak and I want her to sleep."

Margy slipped into the dim room like a shadow. As she approached the bed, Aunt Alice's head turned slightly towards her. Her breathing, though still shallow, was quiet and more regular. Aunt Alice lifted her hand from the coverlet and Margy took it in both of hers. A long look passed between them.

Aunt Alice's voice was a hoarse whisper. "How are you, Margy?"

"I'm fine, Auntalice."

"School going well?"

"Yes, Auntalice."

"Your spelling . . . ?"

"I got a 'B plus' yesterday." (Oh, how she wished she could have reported an "A plus.")

"That's good, dear." (Aunt Alice thinking a "B" was good?)

"Auntalice . . . ," Margy wanted to say a hundred things all at once, but Aunt Alice's eyes were slipping shut, and the nurse was gesturing that it was time for Margy to leave.

Aunt Alice smiled at Margy and squeezed her hand weakly. Margy bent over and kissed her ever so softly on the forehead.

"Sleep tight, Auntalice," she said. "I'll see you in the morning."

CHAPTER
5

A unt Alice's recovery was slow but steady. Each day brought fresh triumphs and Margy could count them off on her fingers: the day Aunt Alice was allowed to sit up for a while, the day the trained nurse left, the day Aunt Alice first came downstairs to sit in the parlour for a few hours and, finally, the Friday night in mid-March when Aunt Alice resumed her rightful place at the head of the table for supper. Aunt Edith cooked a bang-up meal that night to be sure.

Margy rejoiced at Aunt Alice's improvement. It was great fun to be invited to read her the *Times* when she was still confined to her room. It was even rather nice to be drilled in spelling by Aunt Alice again. Best of all was the return of the long talks and discussions that Margy had missed so much.

But Margy never mentioned to Aunt Alice her discovery about Orlie and the shiny American quarter in Mr. Rainer's till. No, Margy's resolve remained firm: she, herself would confront Orlie with her suspicions and find out the Truth. She would show him that she knew what he had done, and wring a confession out of him. She would tell him exactly what she thought of him. And she would do this herself and on her own, just as smart and practical and independent as Aunt Alice.

The trouble was that it was hard to pin Orlie down in the schoolyard or classroom. He was often late for class, or arrived just at the very last minute, and he always left as soon as school was out, hightailing it for his farm home out the Mud Road. At recess or lunch he was perpetually in the midst of a snowball war or some other game, surrounded by a rowdy crowd of pushing and jostling friends. Margy stood along the sidelines, alone or with the faithful Lenore, and watched and waited. But day after day went by and a chance to speak to Orlie never presented itself.

Finally the opportunity came. It was a Friday in early April and Mr. Warren had just announced an important geography test for the coming Monday.

"Be sure you study hard over the weekend," he warned the class. "Every Fourth Form in the country is writing the same examination as a preparation for the 'Entrances' in June. The class with the highest average," (his eyes, alight with the spirit of challenge, swept the class), "the class with the highest average will win a prize donated by the School Boards, and presented in person by one of the trustees: a new wall map of the world. (Heaven knows we need one.) And we might even get our photograph in the *Bancroft Times.*"

The class looked dutifully impressed. A hand waved at the back of the class.

"Yes, George?"

"Sir, what about the people who are away today?" asked George righteously. "They won't study and then when they don't do well on the test, they'll pull the rest of us down." It was clear that George rather fancied having his picture in the paper.

"Yes," said Mr. Warren thoughtfully, "Ruth and Jane and Orlie are all away today. I don't think we need to worry about Ruth . . . ," (mild laughter from the class; Ruth was an excellent student and would no doubt do well without studying at all), "and Cora can take home her book and study with her sister to make sure Jane is ready. But Orlie . . . ."

Everyone knew that Orlie was no scholar, and probably couldn't care less about a geography test even if it meant the class winning a prize.

"Maybe we'll be lucky and Orlie won't show up on Monday," said George, grinning.

"George!" said Mr. Warren in a shocked and reprimanding tone. Education was a profound privilege and not to be taken lightly by anyone, even in jest. Orlie had missed many days of school since Christmas. He told everyone that he had to help his father on the farm but no one knew for sure whether he was simply playing hookey.

Mr. Warren looked perplexed. "Is there anyone who could take Orlie's book to him?" he asked.

Margy felt the hair on the back of her neck stand on end. She forced her hand halfway up. The teacher nodded in her direction.

"I could . . . well, I could take Orlie's book . . . to his house and tell him . . . about the test."

An interested snicker rippled through the classroom. Gwennie made kissing noises on the back of her hand. Margy blushed to the roots of her red hair.

"*That will be enough, Gwenneth,*" said Mr. Warren in a voice like thunder. He turned to Margy. "Thank you, Margy. That would be fine if you could manage to get Orlie's book to him for the weekend. And the rest of you, study hard and we'll have a real chance at the prize. Now . . . take out your penmanship books and do the drill on the blackboard."

As soon as the class was hunched over their penmanship books, Lenore passed a note across the aisle to Margy.

"Are you really going to take Orlie's book to him?"

Margy nodded emphatically.

Lenore's second note said, "Do you want me to go with you?"

Margy shook her head just as emphatically. This was her best chance to get Orlie alone and confront him. Lenore was composing a third note when Mr. Warren came down the aisle to check their work, so she had to hurry into the penmanship exercise instead.

And so it was settled. Margy was to walk out to Orlie Marker's farm on Saturday morning to deliver his geography notebook and exhort him to study for the examination. (Or, if she took George's advice, tell him not to come to school on Monday.)

When Aunt Edith heard Margy's plan after school that night she was indignant. "Surely you don't want to walk all the way out there to the Marker place. It must be a couple of miles out the Mud Road."

Margy shrugged carelessly. "Oh, it's not so far. I'll go tomorrow morning after chores."

"I didn't know that you and the Marker boy were such good friends. 'T.N.O.K.,' you know."

"What's 'T.N.O.K.'?" asked Margy.

Aunt Edith had the grace to look a bit embarrassed. "It means 'They're Not Our Kind,'" she said. "They're not . . . like us. The Markers are . . . very poor."

This didn't make sense to Margy. These days everybody was poor. She said, "But Auntedith, *we're* poor."

Her Aunt looked even more indignant. "Just because we don't have any money does not mean that we're poor." (Margy thought, but that's exactly what it does mean.) Aunt Edith struggled ahead. "It's more about how you live with what you do have. . . . Well, anyway," she finally conceded, "We may be poor, but the Markers are . . . *poor.*"

Margy could see this discussion was going nowhere, and Aunt Alice wasn't around to bail them out, so she simply said, "Orlie and I are not friends; and I *am* going to take his book to him tomorrow morning." She pressed her lips into a thin straight line.

Aunt Edith gave her a long look. "Be careful, Margy," she said. "You look exactly like your Aunt Alice right now."

"Thank you," said Margy.

"That was not intended as a compliment," said Aunt Edith.

Saturday morning dawned chill and overcast. One might almost think that, April notwithstanding, winter was trying to rear its head again for one final snow flurry.

As soon as her morning chores were finished, Margy got ready to leave.

"You're sure you want to do this?" said Aunt Edith.

Margy nodded determinedly and pulled on another sweater.

"Well," said Aunt Edith, "as long as you're going out there, you may as well see if they have any extra eggs for sale. I'll make an angel cake for Sunday dinner." (Angel cake was Aunt Alice's favourite.) "Don't pay more than five cents a dozen, and be sure to ask if they're fresh. Bring me two dozen if they have them."

Margy put Aunt Edith's quarter in her pocket and Orlie's dilapidated notebook in a bag, and headed off down Flint Street. She would like to have taken Bing with her for company, but if the Markers had chickens he might just get carried away and chase them. So best to leave him behind, asleep beside the woodstove in the kitchen.

There was indeed a skiff of snow in the air. Margy pulled her knitted toque a little lower and put her head down into the wind as she turned onto Hastings Street. Just as she passed Cooper's Emporium, the heavy door of the store swung open and Verna, her head down into the wind and dragging her small brother by the hand, ploughed out into the street and smack into Margy. They ended up on their knees on the slippery walkway in front of the store.

Verna recovered first. "Oh, Margy," she said, "Are you all right?"

"I'm fine," said Margy, rubbing her forehead. It was the first time they had spoken for almost three months. Both girls righted themselves and shyly brushed the snow from one another's coats.

Verna glanced over her shoulder towards her father's store. "I miss you so much, Margy," she whispered.

"I miss you too," said Margy miserably. "The club isn't the same without you there. We haven't had hardly any meetings since last Christmas. I mostly just hang around with Lenore now . . . and once in a while Jane and Cora."

"I think the kids in Fourth Form are real mean to you, Margy," said Verna, her whisper rising in anger. "I told 'em you didn't do it. I told my Papa you didn't do it too. But he just wouldn't listen. He said, 'What's bred in the bone,' or some such thing."

"What does that mean?" asked Margy.

"Oh, I don't know," said Verna, pulling her scarf angrily around her neck. "I think it means that your father wasn't from Bancroft so Papa doesn't know what he was like and maybe you're like him."

Margy stared in disbelief at Verna. It was true that her father wasn't from Bancroft and had come from "Out Front" to court Momma. "But my Daddy is a good man," said Margy indignantly.

"Yes, of course he is," said Verna soothingly. "It's just that people around here don't know it because he was 'from away.'" Her voice dropped to a whisper again. "Besides, my Great Aunt Pansy told me that my Papa was sweet on your Ma when they were both young, and he never did like your father much."

Margy stared at Verna in astonishment. How could she ever hope to cut through all the layers of speculation, rumour, and buried feeling in this village to get people to understand the truth?

Verna's small brother Teddy tugged on her sleeve. "Verna, I'm cold."

Verna looked at Margy. Margy looked at Verna.

"Goodbye, Margy. No matter what my Papa says, you'll always be my best friend. He won't always be able to tell me what to do and then we'll be able to see one another again. Someday I'm just going to ignore him and come and visit you. You see if I don't."

Margy didn't know whether to be impressed or dismayed at this fearless rebellion. She put her mittened hand into Verna's. "It may be sooner than you think," she whispered mysteriously.

"Oh, Margy, do you know something that will prove you're innocent?" asked Verna excitedly.

But Margy simply smiled, gave Verna's hand a final encouraging squeeze, and backed away. She turned and headed resolutely up through the bustle of the main street.

Saturday certainly was the day that *everybody* came to town. Margy saw lots of people she knew. Scarcely had she got to the end of the village where the houses thinned out when Gwennie's father in his fancy big car swept past her heading north. Mrs. Jones was sitting proudly in the front seat beside her husband looking every bit the "Duchess of Bancroft" as some people called her behind her back. In the back seat Margy could see Gwennie herself, and beside her . . . *Ralph.*

Where were they going in such pomp and circumstance? And why was Ralph with them?

Gwennie looked straight at Margy as they drove past, then turned and said something to Ralph and laughed. Margy looked down at her shoes and trudged steadily forward, pushing one foot in front of the other. She didn't look up until she was sure Mr. Jones' car would be well around the bend and out of sight.

The Mud Road was aptly named. By the time Margy turned on to it the few snowflakes in the air had melted into the dirt of the roadway to produce a slurry of slush and muck that splashed about her ankles. The farms along the road were few and far between, and much-of-a-muchness: small and run-down with ramshackle outbuildings and houses held together with tarpaper and penny nails.

Finally, when she was almost chilled to the bone, Margy came to a lane with a sign that said "Marker" nailed crookedly to the sagging gate. She turned up the rutted lane and surveyed the "Marker Farm."

It was true what Aunt Edith said. Of all the run-down properties along the Mud Road, this was clear and away one of the runnest-downest. The tiny homestead crouched in a low gully. It had various rooms and additions tacked on in several directions, and a lean-to slapped on the side. Piles of useful odds and ends were stacked carelessly around the little house: here a heap of old tires, there a rusted piece of farm equipment (or was it the innards of an old car?). In front of the small building a faded Union Jack nailed to a stubby flag pole shouted a certain proud defiance to the world.

The only signs of life were the few scrawny chickens scratching in the mud around the door, and a wisp of sullen smoke escaping from the leaning chimney. Margy walked boldy up to the door and knocked firmly.

Two girls a bit younger but with exactly the same freckles as Orlie opened the door and stood inside, their mouths agape at this unexpected company.

"Could I speak to Orlie, please?" said Margy. The two girls said nothing but continued to stare at her. Two smaller brothers appeared at their elbows.

Margy tried again. "I brought Orlie his geography book so he could study for the test on Monday."

The four all began to talk at once, their voices rising in shrill competition, their arms waving in wild gesticulation. Suddenly Mrs. Marker appeared behind them in the doorway and sent the whole pack of them scattering noisily back into the house.

"Now, ain't this nice," she said cordially. "We don't get much company out this way. Won't you come in and sit a spell?"

She drew Margy into the main room of the small house. Sweeping a pile of clothing and papers off the end of a dilapidated chesterfield, she plumped up a gaudy red and yellow velvet cushion that had the word "Mother" painted on it, indicating that Margy should take this seat of honour. Margy was grateful to "rest her bones" after the long walk, and also to get into the murky warmth of the small house.

Mrs. Marker sat in a large rocking chair before the open fireplace. "So you're a friend of Orland's, dropping in to visit him. Ain't that nice? Orland is out, working on the farm with his father, but they'll be in soon. We're all going into town this afternoon to do our Saturday trading."

The four children clustered around their mother and began simultaneously to explain to her who Margy was and why she was there. Again Mrs. Marker sent them scattering and silenced them by outshouting the lot. They contented themselves with buzzing noisily in the background, talking and laughing and poking at one another until Margy thought she'd go crazy from the noise and confusion in the small room.

Mrs. Marker settled in for a good visit. "So you're Margy Mullett," she said. "Orland has often spoken of you."

"Margy Stratton," said Margy faintly.

"Well, he'll be real pleased to see you," Mrs. Marker went on as if she had scarcely heard her. "He's missed a lot of school lately . . . but his pa needed a lot of help running a spread this size." Margy wondered what there could possibly be to keep Mr. Marker and Orlie busy on this miserable little farm but of course she nodded her head politely.

The four children were getting steadily more rambunctious, and their mother shouted at them once again to settle down. "They're excited about going to town," she said apologetically. She reached out and cuffed one good-naturedly on the ear as he roared past.

"That there's Archibald," she said fondly, "And the othern's Launcelot. The girls are Veronica and Lorelei." (Margy remarked to herself how odd it was that the plainest families often gave their children the fanciest names.) "Cline and Raymond are off helping their uncle." Mrs. Marker glanced around distractedly. "I think that's all."

"No, no! Little Sammy! Little Sammy!" four voices chorused.

Mrs. Marker laughed. "Yes, of course. Little Sammy."

She gestured towards a secluded and rather dark nook of the small room. For the first time Margy noticed a little boy, perhaps four years old, sitting on the floor. He was almost out of sight behind a dilapidated armchair and seemed oblivious to the melee around him. In front of him on the floor he had lined up a row of assorted jars, each partly full of water, and was contentedly plinking on them with a short stick, although how he could hear anything over the ruckus was beyond Margy.

"That's our Little Sammy all right," said Mrs. Marker. "He's so quiet he usually gets forgotten." She laughed comfortably. "Once we were halfway home from town before we realized we'd left him behind. Had to go all the way back to fetch him."

Archibald (or was it Launcelot?) tore past Little Sammy's corner and upset two of the water jars and the small boy as well. Little Sammy let out an inarticulate roar and lunged at the jars to right them before the water ran out.

"Here now, Sammy. You ain't kilt." Mrs. Marker lumbered over and righted the child. "Samuel's the youngest," she said, rather unnecessarily to Margy. Margy looked at her thickening figure and thought to herself, but not for much longer.

"And of course Orland, as you know, is the oldest," Mrs. Marker continued. "You know him from school, don't you dear?" Mrs. Marker was evidently on to a favourite subject. "Orland is such a help to his father, such a good boy. Why, in December he did a lot of odd jobs in town and brought me the money he earned to make a real nice Christmas for the young ones." She glanced lovingly at the gaudy cushion on the chesterfield. "He bought me that beautiful gift with his own earnings."

I bet, thought Margy. *I just bet.*

The small clock on a corner shelf rang twelve-thirty. Mrs. Marker looked at Margy and said, "I'd invite you to take a bit of lunch but we ate early owing to us going to town this afternoon." The four older children looked startled and dismayed at this remark and Launcelot (or was it Archibald?) started to say something but was silenced by a glare from his mother. "Would you take a cup of tea though, dear?"

"Thank you, Mrs. Marker," said Margy politely, "But I ate just before I came." (It was characteristic of this Great Depression, she thought, that Mrs. Marker would tell that "white" falsehood simply because she didn't have any food to feed a guest, and that she herself would tell an equal falsehood in response to save face as well, and that even scrupulously honest Aunt Alice would have faulted neither.) "I really just came to see Orlie and bring him his geography book." Then she remembered, "And to buy some eggs for my Aunt Edith."

All four of the older children made a stampede to the lean-to to retrieve some fresh eggs, until with all the shouting and pushing Margy felt she would be surprised if there were one single egg in the paper bag left unbroken. The money changed hands and there were congenial smiles all around.

Then Mrs. Marker said, "Margy, why don't you just step out and beyond the barn. Orland and his Pa are digging post holes back there. We're building a bigger pen for our cow, now that spring is here."

"Yes," said Margy with relief. "I'll just do that." She was glad for an oppportunity to escape from the noise and confusion of the house.

"Tell Mr. Marker that we're well nigh ready to go to town," Mrs. Marker called after her as she crossed the yard.

The "barn" was a small shed just past a clump of brush. Beyond that Margy found Mr. Marker and Orlie struggling to centre a post in the dark muck.

Mr. Marker looked up. "Say, Orlie. Here's your girl." He nudged Orlie with his elbow and gave him a broad wink. Margy felt her face go red.

"Mrs. Marker asked me to tell you that she's about ready to go to town," she said.

Mr. Marker straightened his back and dug a pocket watch out of his trousers. "Well, I'll just leave you two alone then." Again the sly nudge and wink at Orlie who looked as embarrassed as Margy felt.

Then Mr. Marker's face grew hard. "Orlie, you'll finish off them post holes before I get back or I'll know the reason why."

"Aw, Pa. Don't I get to go to town? The guys are meeting at the . . ."

His father pushed the shovel into his hand. "Didn't you hear me, boy? Them post holes got to be dug. Now, get at it." He turned on his heel and walked away towards the house.

Orlie's thin shoulders drooped. Margy would have felt sorry for him if she hadn't been so pleased at the turn of events that finally put her alone with him. The two contemplated one another for a few long moments.

Finally, "I brought your geography book so as you could study for the test on Monday," she said.

"Fat chance," replied Orlie cheerfully. "Fat chance that I'll get these darn post holes finished by then." (Margy thought, well, at least George will be happy.)

"Orlie . . ." Margy had waited so long for this moment, and now she didn't know quite where to begin.

Finally she plunged in. "Orlie, did you take our class Christmas Cheer money from the school?"

There, it was said.

Orlie took a half step back and the grin faded from his face. "What makes you say that?" he asked evasively, a guarded look dropping over his eyes.

"Orlie, I *know* you took the money."

"And just how do you know that, Margy Stratton?" said Orlie in a cocksure but slightly forced voice.

"Because my Aunt Alice gave me a special quarter to put in the jar . . . *and you spent that very same quarter at Mr. Rainer's store a few days later.*" Margy's voice was quiet but dead sure.

Orlie said nothing for a moment. Then, in a slow and wooden tone, as if he had said the same thing to himself many times before, "That money was collected for a poor family at Christmas and it just so happens a poor family did get it and use it. And they had a real nice Christmas with it." He looked Margy defiantly in the eye and closed his mouth firmly as if no more needed to be said on the matter.

"Or-leeee," Margy's voice was a wail, "You've got to go to Mr. Warren and tell him you took it."

Orlie's voice took on a reasoning tone. "Look, I'd

like to help you out, Margy, but I can't. Why, if my Pa ever heard that I'd taken that money he'd cane me near to death, or else just pure kick me out. And my Ma would just about die of shame. So I *can't* tell. Besides, everybody's most forgotten by now."

"No, they haven't 'most forgotten,'" said Margy loudly, stamping her foot and sending a splash of mud in all directions. "They haven't forgotten *at all.*" Three months of agonizing loneliness echoed in her voice.

"Sorry, Margy. I won't tell Mr. Warren or anybody . . . and you'd better not try telling them any such thing either." Orlie's small thin face was so white with stubbornness and defiance that even his freckles had disappeared. He glanced in the direction of the house and his voice was hard. "You'd better go if you want to get a ride back into town with my folks." Then he deliberately turned his back on Margy and started to pace off the number of steps for the next post hole.

Margy felt hot tears sting behind her eyelids. She shook them angrily away and glared after Orlie.

"Orlie Marker," she said loudly, not caring who heard her, *"Orlie Marker, you are a dirty sneaking little coward."*

She spun on her heel and marched towards the house where the entire Marker clan were excitedly scrambling themselves into the ancient truck for the trip to town. When she glanced over her shoulder she could see Orlie, his back to the wind, his thin shoulders hunched over the shovel, scrabbling in the half-frozen mud.

Margy was very quiet for the trip back to town, crammed into the back of the truck up against the silent Little Sammy, protecting Aunt Edith's eggs from the other four children who jostled and frolicked around her. She went over the afternoon in her mind.

She had seen Orlie, confronted him, and as much as heard him confess. And she had told him exactly what she thought of him. Then why did she now feel worse than ever?

And the Lonely Time ground on.

CHAPTER
—6—

The following Monday dawned bright and cheery, a stark contrast to Margy's spirits. Orlie Marker did not show up at school; the class did not win the Board prize anyway.

Orlie finally appeared in class on Wednesday, halfway through the morning, making an entrance as usual. He studiously avoided Margy—until they accidentally ended up beside each other in the line for recess. He turned towards her but his eyes shifted away whenever she looked at him. And when their eyes finally did meet he gave her a half-afraid, half-challenging look that seemed to say, *"I dare you to say anything to anybody."*

With the rest of the class he was just as perky and brash as ever. That very day he nicked an apple from Ralph Phillips' lunch box and ate it right in front of him. And everybody just thought it was funny and laughed at him.

Day followed day, week followed week. Margy went through the humdrum motions of life. Breakfast, school, lunch, school, chores, supper, homework, walk Bing, go to bed.

Sometimes there was a shaft of sunlight through the

cloud of loneliness. Like the time Jane and Cora invited Margy to their house after school to see their new kittens. It was almost like old times.

But then right after that, the next day in fact, Margy was chosen dead last for the Friday spelling bee. Lenore said it was just because Margy wasn't very good in spelling, but Margy knew differently.

At least at home things were almost back to normal, "things" meaning Aunt Alice. She was back working at her beloved library again now, fretting over the "mess and mayhem" created by the volunteers from the Library Board who had taken over during her illness. She also had to catch up on reading the books that had arrived over the past several months. Aunt Alice made a point of reading every single volume before she put it on the shelf of the Bancroft Public Library. That way, she could discard any books that she felt were unsuitable, or at the very least, black out the offending words with India ink before anyone else had to read them. Aunt Alice took her job at the library very seriously indeed.

Once the library was back in order and running smoothly again, Aunt Alice turned her attention towards the Fine House and the annual ritual of Spring Housecleaning. Margy, having experienced this tradition the previous year, knew that the time had come when Aunt Alice announced at breakfast one Saturday in early May that their hired man would be in that week to "do the pipes."

It was really the worst day of the whole year. Both Aunts would be crabby for hours before it happened, during the procedure and for hours afterwards. To make matters worse, this year it was to happen on a Tuesday. Tuesday, the very day Aunt Edith did her special baking for the week. There would be no lemon meringue pie, no tomato soup cake with cream cheese icing.

Stovepipe cleaning day! Why oh why hadn't Margy thought to hint to Lenore to be invited to her house after school in the hopes that the mess would all be over by the time she got home. But when she came through the door after school on Tuesday night they were still into it, with wet sooty newspapers spread all around the kitchen, and everyone giving advice or shouting instructions and no one listening. Such a botheration about nothing, thought Margy.

But Aunt Alice insisted that it be done, every spring without fail. Each stovepipe must be taken down and thoroughly cleaned, and the chimneys burnt out, so that there would be no danger of fire in them the following winter. And the messy process was a necessary prerequisite to Spring Housecleaning. That was to commence bright and early on Wednesday morning, the twenty-fourth of May, Queen Victoria's birthday notwithstanding. Margy would be home from school that day and would be "such a help," according to Aunt Edith.

> "'The twenty-fourth of May
> Is the Queen's birthday;
> And if you don't give us a holiday
> We'll all run away,'"

Margy quoted darkly to Aunt Edith.

"But don't you see, Margy," explained the Aunt patiently, "it *will* be a holiday for you because you'll be doing something *different* instead of going to school. 'A change is as good as a rest.'" (Aunt Edith had a pithy maxim for every occasion.) "Besides, if we get a good early start, you might still be able to take in part of the Victoria Day picnic."

"We could leave the housecleaning until the weekend and all go to the picnic," said Margy hopefully.

"Absolutely not," decreed Aunt Alice. "We've left it late enough. The bushes are in bud already and the garden must be planted 'when the lilac leaves are as big as a mouse's ear.'" (Aunt Alice had an equal storehouse of maxims.) "So the Spring Housecleaning must begin." Aunt Alice's voice sounded as strong and determined as it did before her illness and Margy was glad to hear it, even though she knew that when her Aunt used that tone it was folly to argue.

Margy consoled herself with thoughts of the picnic. Last year it had been such fun, with a programme of singing, a patriotic address by the United Church minister on "The Life and Example of our Late Queen," a football match, and a five-mile race. Snuffy Farrow had beat all the other fellows last year, coming across the finish line in thirty-one and a quarter minutes, but Margy sure would like to see how she could do against that time if they would let a girl enter the race. Yes indeed, the Twenty-Fourth of May picnic certainly would have been the "carrot at the end of the stick" to encourage Margy to work as hard as she could all day long.

This year, of course, would be different. She and

Lenore would go together but Margy would hang back on the sidelines watching the fun instead of being in the thick of it. Maybe she and Lenore would try for the Girls' Three-legged Race, but they were so sadly mismatched, Margy's tall thin frame to Lenore's dumpling short-legged one, that winning was unlikely. Last year they had ended in a heap halfway to the finish line. But the boys had cheered their attempt anyway, and Ralph and Snuffy had jumped out from the sidelines to untangle them and help them up. That had made it well worth losing the race, for both girls. Maybe, Margy thought, we could lose the race again this year and see if they would help us up again. Margy could feel her cheeks go a comfortable pink at the thought.

Aunt Alice's voice brought her sharply back to the present. "Now there is no reason that three people working diligently together cannot make a good start on the housecleaning if they put their minds and backs into it. We'll do the upstairs today and the downstairs on Saturday." She went on to describe to Margy the airing of pillows and bedding, turning of mattresses, washing of woodwork, wiping out of the light fixtures, and everything else that was involved in what she referred to as "deep cleaning." "If we need a carpet carried out to the backyard to beat, we'll give you a call, Margy."

Margy nodded. "Yes, Auntalice."

"In the meantime," (as if she were designating a Special Honour), "you can do the laundry as we send it down. Thank goodness it's a fine sunny day for drying blankets. Do you think you can handle it on your own? It's a big job."

Margy nodded again. She had helped both Aunts do the laundry dozens of times. It would be a challenge to do it all on her own but she would show the Aunts what a splendid job she could make of it. Besides, doing anything was better than sitting around thinking about the picnic she was missing. Perhaps when the laundry was done she would slip over to the picnic grounds and see if she could find Lenore.

The Aunts, laden with mops, brooms, pails and rags, disappeared up the stairs whence laundry soon began to appear in the form of doilies, antimacassars, ruffled curtains, mattress covers, and several heavy wool blankets. Margy quickly rinsed and stacked the few breakfast dishes—deal with them later when the laundry was well under way—and dragged the washing machine in from the summer kitchen.

What a wonderful invention was the washing machine, and this one was a particular beauty. It was Aunt Alice's "pride and joy," even more than the radio in the parlour, and had been bought for her by Grandfather not long before he died. The machine was a shining white, electrical model with an attached electric wringer. Why, with a modern convenience like this, there was almost no work at all involved in doing the laundry.

Once the washing machine was positioned in the middle of the kitchen floor, with the rinse tub and laundry basket on the bench table beside it, Margy filled the washer with hot water from the large copper boiler on the back of the woodstove, pouring it by the saucepan full through the soap sieve to make it nice and sudsy. Thrifty Aunt Edith kept all the little ends of soap in this screened utensil to use up on laundry day.

As soon as the washer was filled and ready, Margy put in the first load of sorted "whites" and turned the handle to begin the determined swish of the agitator. Then she refilled the copper boiler from the rain barrel so that she could boil the linen dresser scarves and napkins on the back of the stove. By the time she filled the rinse tub she was ready to pull the first load out of the washer and through the rollers into the clear rinse water. Despite her low spirits, Margy found herself taking quiet pleasure in feeding the sheets between the tight rollers that squeezed the hot soapy water back into the washer, all the while taking care not to get her fingers tangled in the fabric and pulled into the rollers. Margy felt she was accomplishing her assigned task with speed and efficiency and it gave her a certain sense of pride and independence. Her spirits began to lift somewhat.

Just when she thought she had the system working perfectly Margy remembered that the "whites" should have bluing added to their rinse water. So she had to go back and do the first lot again, this time swishing the little cheesecloth bag filled with bluing crystals through the water. Not too much though, or instead of making the whites whiter it would give them a bluish tinge, the sure sign of a sloppy housekeeper.

Then there were those few items that should be starched, the dresser scarves and doilies. Margy mixed up the corn starch and cold water in the big yellow bowl. By the time she got it to the right consistency she had way too much. No matter. Aunt Edith always ended up with too much and just set aside the extra for a lovely blanc mange pudding for supper. (It was remarkable to Margy that the self-same starch that made crisp collars and cuffs could, with the simple addition of butter, brown sugar, vanilla and a sprinkle of coconut, be made into a perfectly delicious dessert.) In any case, corn starch and cold water, stir in the boiling water, dip in the dresser scarves and doilies, and presto! The first load was ready to hang out on the clothesline in the backyard.

Margy carried the heavy basket out to the yard and set it down on the grass. She was glad it was Wednesday and not a regular Monday wash day. It was a matter of pride to be the first in the neighbourhood to have her washing billowing on the line where everyone could see and appreciate the industry and efficiency of the lady of the house. By now it was close to nine-thirty and Margy knew she would not have been first had this been a Monday. She did not, however, have any qualms about the whiteness of her whites, and felt that they could hold their own in comparison with anyone in the village.

Margy poked five clothes pegs into her mouth and stepped up to the line. It was a strange-looking clothesline, rather like a giant umbrella that had got itself blown inside out in the wind, its wooden spokes pointing up and the lines going between them like a big square spider's web. The advantage to this kind of clothesline, as Aunt Edith had often pointed out, was that one could hang her nicest items on the outside for the passing world to see, and conceal her older, tattier, mended items (or personal clothing like underwear) on the very inside, away from the probing eyes of the public. Margy was careful to hang only the best sheets and the pillow slips with the crocheted edges on the outside, and the striped mattress cover within.

The dresser scarves and doilies she spread carefully on the grass where the sunlight would shine on them directly and bleach them. Aunt Alice swore by sunlight as the most gentle way to bleach linens, while Aunt Edith declared that moonlight was *so* much better. This was an issue of prolonged debate between the Aunts, but since sunlight was what was available in quantity right now, sunlight was what they got.

Margy worked steadily, interrupted only by Aunt Edith tossing more little piles of laundry from the top of the stairs as they moved from room to room. None of the things looked all that dirty to Margy but Aunt Alice had pointed out earlier that the very same soot that had been inside those dreadful stovepipes was also deposited in a thin film over everything in the house, from curtains to coverlets to carpets. And it was the same in every house in Bancroft—in Canada even— that heated all winter with coal or wood. And if the house weren't cleaned thoroughly every spring without fail, then the next year everything would be twice as dingy, and so on until it became *permanent.* Aunt Alice said "permanent" in a tone that implied "fatal."

They took a break for lunch and the Aunts examined Margy's work thus far. Why, she had even remembered to bring the starched items in when they were just the right degree of dampness, and had "rolled them down" and put them in the icebox to await ironing the next day.

"Look at that washing machine," said Aunt Alice, a proud glint in her eye. She stuck her hand into the soapy water, then withdrew it quickly. "The water is still piping hot. That's because of the double stainless steel tub. Keeps the water hot forever." She savoured a final sip of tea. "Remember that, Margy," she said. "Always buy *quality*. It pays for itself in the long run."

"Well, back to work." Aunt Edith set her teacup down. "You finish off that quilt and blanket, Margy, and that will be enough for today. You've done extremely well with your job."

This rare praise shot a ray of sunshine into Margy's gloomy heart. After the Aunts left the kitchen she attacked the lunch dishes while the quilt washed. Then she put the blanket into the tub and turned the handle to start the agitator. Margy was about to take the quilt out to hang on the line when there was an urgent knock on the back door and Cora Parker's face popped in.

"C'mon, Margy," said Cora urgently. "There's a big log jam in the river and they're going to try to break it."

Margy hesitated, but only for a second. She longed for a taste of the Victoria Day festivities, even if it was just a quick peek at the log jam in the river. After all, hadn't Aunt Edith said she was doing "extremely well" with her job? The Aunts were busy washing woodwork upstairs and were unlikely to come down. If they called and she didn't answer they would just assume that she was out in the backyard hanging up laundry. What difference would it make if she left for just ten minutes and took a quick look? Margy whipped off her apron and followed the breathless Cora out the kitchen door, closing it softly behind them. They skirted the house, collected Bing who was sleeping in the sunshine on the front porch, and made a dash down the hill towards the river. Margy hoped that one of the Aunts didn't happen to be looking out an upstairs window at that exact moment.

Quite a large crowd, at least three dozen people, had clustered on the bridge and along the banks of the York River which was running fast and high. Every spring when the snow melted the river rose and flooded its banks, turning Hastings Street into a river of its own. By late May the river had usually settled back into its peaceful and picturesque natural state, and it stayed that way all summer—except when they opened the dam farther up at Baptiste Lake to bring the log drives through.

Simply having a drive go through the village was exciting enough. Dozens of river drivers, the "rough riders," would descend all at once upon Bancroft, one of the few towns along the river system. The hotels and boarding houses, the bank, the barber shop and the tobacco shop, Rainer's Hardware and Cooper's Emporium would all hum with activity. Why, it was reported that hundreds, maybe thousands, of dollars went through the Post Office in Bancroft as the married river drivers sent their pay back to their families in the communities "from away." As for the unmarried river drivers, well, many a Bancroft mother warned her pretty marriage-aged daughters about those good-looking, fast-talking, loose-spending men who "drove the river."

Yes, the advent of a log drive was exciting in itself, but a log jam was a whole new story. (Margy had heard many tales the year before in Junior Fourth from boys who themselves fancied the exciting life of a river drover.) The winding, treacherous journey made by the trees that were felled above Bancroft on Baptiste Lake to the lumber mills at Arnprior took two full years. Jam-ups were an inevitable occurrence, calling out every ounce of wit and skill the river drivers possessed in order to resolve the jam quickly, efficiently, and without loss of life. Too often they ended with an unmarked grave in the wilderness beside a tight bend in the river. And a short letter from the River Boss to a distant grieving family, using phrases like "good worker" and "well liked by all the men," enclosing the man's back pay and maybe a few dollars extra if The Company allowed.

Margy and Cora wiggled their way between the people lining the bridge. Too late she discovered that she was standing right beside Ralph, pushed right up against him in fact. He simply grinned at her and said enthusiastically, "Some show, Margy," indicating the log jam.

She nodded, looking at him, not the river.

"You coming to the picnic later?"

Margy nodded again. *(Oh, why wouldn't her voice say something clever and interesting?)*

Ralph seemed pleased. "You want to meet up with us there?"

Margy nodded a third time, very enthusiastically. *(He must think I'm a proper idiot, just nodding up and down like a dummy.)*

"Good," said Ralph. "George and Orlie and Gwennie are meeting me at the main gate at three. We'll watch for you."

Margy did not nod this time. She said, "Huh!" in a very unladylike way.

A shout drew their attention to the river just downstream from the bridge. There, just where the river made a slight curve and went through the open dam by the mill, lay a tangle of logs packed solidly across the waterway, but still shifting and seething as if anxious to break free and be on its way. Several of the river drivers had ventured out on the twisted mass, each man stepping cautiously from log to log, probing with his long hooked pike pole for the "jam dog." This was the one special log that was the key to releasing all the rest and which, once loosened, would set the whole log boom free to continue its course down the river.

Evidently they had found that all-important log, for two men gingerly drove an iron ring into one end of it and threaded a rope through the ring. As the watching crowd held its collective breath the men retreated cautiously to the safety of the shore and a group of drovers pulled on the rope to draw the log out from the tangled heap. After much pulling and shouting on the part of the men the log slipped out—but the jam held fast. A groan went up from the watching crowd, which by now had swelled to over fifty people.

The Drive Boss himself clambered out onto the jam, selected another possible jam dog, and the process began again. The spectators grew even more quiet, knowing that should the jam break up spontaneously, the men who were out on it would have to "go with it," jumping to the biggest log handy and hanging on for dear life, balancing with their pike poles while the released boom bucked and plunged through the narrow dam opening.

This second effort, however, met with success. With a mighty grinding and crunching sound, the jam broke in a thundering, rolling release with all the river drivers safely ashore. A cheer went up from the crowd, and the river men waved triumphantly in the direction of the bridge.

"See ya later," said Ralph cheerfully, and wandered off to talk to one of the river drivers.

Cora was still jumping up and down in one spot from sheer excitement. "Oh, Margy, wasn't that *great?*" She saucily threw a kiss to one of the handsome drovers below.

"Cora!" said Margy, shocked.

Cora shrugged. "You want to go down to the Emporium to get some 'bull's eyes'?" she asked. "I've got a nickel." Then she realized what she'd said and turned a sympathetic crimson.

Margy hadn't been inside Cooper's Emporium since the day she picked out Aunt Alice's Wonderful Gift. It was great that Cora had asked her to come and see the log jam and to invite her to go down street and buy a treat. Cora wasn't exactly a Best Friend of the status of the loyal Lenore or the exiled Verna. Still, she and Jane were good friends and members of the Order of the White Cloud, and they had been kind about the kittens. And Ralph had talked to her today and invited her to come to the picnic with him and George. Maybe Orlie was right; maybe people were beginning to forget about the accusation that had cast a cloud over her name.

Then Margy thought about Gwennie and her pencil business, and about the terribly distant feeling she still had at school in spite of the friendship of Lenore and Jane and Cora. And Margy knew that she would *never* go into Cooper's Emporium again, and have those snooty salesladies and Verna's sisters watching her. No, never, not even when she was rich and famous someday and old Mr. Cooper himself begged her to come into his store. Margy knew in her heart of hearts that people hadn't forgotten but that she was simply becoming so used to the Lonely Time that it seemed normal now.

"I'd better be getting home," she said slowly and Cora nodded understandingly. Margy whistled for Bing and turned. Then she realized quite suddenly that she really *had* to be getting home. It was far more than ten minutes since she had come to "take a quick look." Margy headed off at a dead run.

She streaked through the kitchen door, not pausing to worry if it slammed this time. Aunt Edith was in the kitchen, shaking her head over the blanket she had just put through the ringer.

"Look at that, Alice. Shrunk beyond recognition. And one of our good blankets too. Off *my* bed." She spread out the pathetic item. It looked thick and matted, and much smaller than Margy remembered. Hardly big enough for Bing's little bed now.

Aunt Alice looked Margy up and down severely. "Whatever possessed you to go off and leave a good wool blanket in that hot water for so long?"

"There was a log jam in the river," began Margy bravely, "And Cora Parker . . ."

"A log jam!" interrupted Aunt Alice sharply. "Was anyone hurt?"

"No, Auntalice. It sure was some swell though, the way they broke it up by 'pulling the jam dog.'" Perhaps if she could get Aunt Alice sidetracked on the exciting details of the afternoon the ruined blanket would be forgotten.

Surprisingly Aunt Alice did not stay to hear the "exciting details." She set her lips into a thin white line and turned on her heel. They heard her slow footsteps mount the stairs and her bedroom door close quietly.

Margy looked questioningly at Aunt Edith, who shook her head sadly. After a pause she spoke.

"A long time ago," Aunt Edith explained in a soft voice, "I think it was in '07 or '08—your Aunt Alice was about seventeen and I was just a little girl a lot younger than you are now—anyway, there was a terrible log jam in the river at the dam by the mill. The river drivers did everything they could think of to break it up but it wouldn't move. Then the Drive Boss announced that The Company would give a twenty-dollar gold piece to any of the local men who could draw the jam dog. Of course there were lots willing to try, but the three who did it were the McKenzie boys, James, Kenneth, and Robert."

Aunt Edith had a far-away look in her eyes. "I think that your Aunt Alice . . . well, she thought a good deal of Robert McKenzie. People called him 'her beau,' and he did give her a pearl ring." (Margy knew that ring! Aunt Alice kept it in a tiny velvet-lined box in the top drawer of her chiffonnier.) "Of course your Grandfather wouldn't let them become engaged because he said

Alice was too young. But they did have 'an understanding.' And she told your mother and me that Robert was going to give her a real engagement ring for her eighteenth birthday."

Margy's eyes sparkled. Fancy Aunt Alice having a real beau! And imagine how proud she would feel when he did something so brave and honourable as break the log jam. Just the same as she would feel if Ralph were to be the hero of the day and bring glory to himself and the village.

Aunt Edith went on, "And I was going to be the bridesmaid and wear a blue dress and have my hair up. And Lizzy was going to stand up for her too. It didn't matter what Pa said." With difficulty Aunt Edith pulled herself back to the thread of the story. "Yes, the McKenzie boys broke the jam all right." Her voice grew even softer and she glanced towards the kitchen door and the stairs. "They found James' and Kenneth's bodies a mile or so downstream. What chance did they have when it broke up underneath them, and them inexperienced and all. They never found Robert's body. Old Mrs. McKenzie keeps the twenty-dollar gold piece on the mantle in her parlour. She's never spent it, not even a few years ago when they almost lost their farm."

"Oh," said Margy in a quiet voice.

"There were one or two other beaus later," said Aunt Edith, "but it was never the same for Alice. Robert McKenzie was . . . well, Robert was *Robert."*

Margy nodded understandingly and glanced at the door through which Aunt Alice had disappeared so abruptly.

"When you're young," sighed Aunt Edith, "you

think that nothing bad can ever happen to you, only to the other fellow."

As she hung the tiny matted blanket on the line in the backyard, Margy thought about what Aunt Edith had said. Margy was young, but she knew that bad things could happen to her. Why, Momma had died. And then Daddy had got married again and had to send her away. Now Margy was living with such a cloud of suspicion over her that she couldn't even enjoy the Victoria Day picnic. On the contrary, thought Margy, *everything* bad seems to happen to me.

Then she thought about the log jam long ago, about old Mrs. McKenzie and her twenty-dollar gold piece, about Aunt Alice and Robert McKenzie. And about the little pearl ring, safe in its velvet box upstairs.

Bad things, thought Margy, happen to *everybody*.

CHAPTER
—7—

June was the crazy month for the Senior Fourths.

For many in Margy's class their school days were winding down. They would not be back for high school in the fall. And it seemed as if these last days of June were their final chance to attempt every single prank that had ever entered their minds.

Mr. Warren patiently ran the gamut of their inventiveness: the spitball made from blotting paper and aimed at the back of his head while he was writing on the board, the rolled-up wall maps loaded with broken chalk, the garter snake in his desk drawer (ever so much more effective with a woman teacher).

By mid-June he was bodily ejecting the worst pranksters from his room and keeping the lesser offenders writing lines on the blackboard by the hour. ("'I will not glue Lenore Spencer's desk shut with chewing gum' one hundred times, Mister Farrow, before you may leave.") The in-betweens felt the sting of the teacher's strap, the number of strokes depending on the severity of the crime.

Margy was aware of the panorama of pranks around her. But she was not a part of any of them. Oh, she had lots of good ideas and would have loved to try them out or pass them on to bolder souls than herself. But she spent her time as she had for the whole term, bent over her desk, quietly doing her work, trying to stay as inconspicuous as possible. She never put up her hand any more to volunteer an answer. And when it had been her turn to recite her Robert Service poems for Memory Work in front of the class, she had done it as quickly and with as little expression as possible, and then hurried back to her desk. Nevertheless, she did enjoy the practical jokes that were going off like firecrackers in the classroom, most originating from the back of the room where George and Snuffy and . . . certain other people sat.

The crowning moment of glory occurred when Mr. Warren found that the classroom strap, which he kept in the private bottom drawer of his desk, had been painted a bright yellow, with the words "Old Man Warren" in large crude black letters. Truly this was one exploit that would go down in the history of the Bancroft Public School, and be held up as an example of what a person could accomplish if he really put his mind to it.

When the teacher discovered the exact same shade of yellow paint under one of Orlie Marker's fingernails, Orlie pleaded "circumstantial evidence." This was a phrase that had come into popular use several years earlier when Captain Lindberg's baby son was stolen and murdered, and the kidnapper identified only by suggestive facts surrounding the case. Orlie's protestations did him no more good than the Lindberg kidnapper, however, for he was the first to taste the sting (five strokes, each hand) of the redecorated strap.

To Margy's disgust the whole class rose up to praise Orlie as a kind of hero-martyr, with the girls in Senior Fourth falling over one another trying to express their admiration for this daring and entertaining exploit.

Gwennie, who had never so much as given Orlie the time of day, said right out loud in front of the whole class (when Mr. Warren was out of the room), "Orlie Marker, you're just such a 'smart apple' I don't know what we'll do with you."

Does *no one*, thought Margy, see a certain parallel between stealing the strap out of Mr. Warren's desk drawer and the missing Christmas Cheer money? But before she could decide how to drop a hint about a possible connection between the two Gwennie discovered a dead mouse in her desk, and the fuss she made about it diverted the whole class in another direction.

Yes, for some in the class, June was an entertaining and light-hearted conclusion to their academic career. On the other hand, for those who were hoping to come back in the fall to Continuation School, June was a month of hard work and nervous tension. Preparation for the dreaded "Entrance Examinations" was in full swing. For weeks the scholars crammed history and geography, literature and composition, arithmetic, penmanship, spelling, and especially grammar.

"To make studying more fun" Mr. Warren arranged a contest: the prize of a brand-new red pencil to the person in Senior Fourth who could find the longest sentence and parse it—provided only that they bring the book they found it in as proof it really existed in

English literature. Aunt Alice found a sentence for Margy to enter in the contest: it was from her Prayer Book and had one hundred and seventy-one words in it, twenty-three commas, four semi-colons, and two full colons. It took Margy three and a half hours to parse it:

'Almighty'   — adjective, modifying the noun 'God';

'God'   — proper noun, vocative case;

'Our'   — possessive adjective, modifying 'Father';

'Heavenly'   — adjective, modifying the noun 'Father';

'Father'   — referring back to noun 'God', part of adjective phrase modifying 'God';

'Who'   — pronoun, subject of the adjective phrase . . .

Margy won the red pencil. Mr. Warren seemed very pleased, and made a short speech in presenting it to her in front of the class, displaying her pages of neat writing and the Prayer Book as proof of the validity of her win. There was a smattering of applause. After all, the next longest sentence had only thirty-two words in it. Even so, when the class was getting their coats on to go out for recess a few minutes later, Gwennie took the opportunity to hiss at Margy, "Teacher's pet! Teacher's pet!"

Margy didn't want to be the teacher's pet exactly, but she did want Mr. Warren to like her because she thought a good deal of him. Hadn't he been kind to her ever since that first day she joined the class well over a year ago, when he had told her that marguerites were his favourite flower? She had always felt that he was somehow on her side, and she did not want to leave school with him believing that she might have had anything to do with the missing money.

To tell him about Orlie, or not? Margy went back and forth a dozen times a day. She would still *not* ask Aunt Alice; she would face the thing squarely on her own.

If she told, Orlie would probably deny it. He would probably plead "circumstantial evidence" again. But what if Mr. Warren believed Margy's story anyway? Orlie would get into terrible trouble with his father, who truly was "as hard as flint and mean as rat poison" like everybody said. And maybe the police would be called in and take Orlie off to prison. People tended to look down on the poor people who lived out the Mud Road. What chance would Orlie and his family have if the community turned on them?

Orlie's real friends (and the popular prankster had many) would never forgive Margy for squealing on him, and she might just as well get used to living in the Lonely Time for the rest of her life, or as long as she lived in Bancroft.

But wasn't it unfair to be punished for something Orlie did just because she spoke up to clear her own name? Aunt Edith always said that "Virtue is its own reward." Well, maybe "sin was its own punishment" as well; if you steal something you should expect to be treated like a thief.

But then Margy remembered the proud look on Mrs. Marker's face when she pointed out the "Mother" cushion Orlie had bought her for Christmas. Margy could imagine the look on her face when her eldest son, her pride and joy, was marched off by Constable Palmer. And what about those younger brothers and sisters of Orlie's who would have to go all the way through school in the shadow of their brother?

But just when Margy had decided for sure that she could not tell on Orlie, she would hear Aunt Alice's voice in her head saying, "Truth and honesty, first and foremost," and she would swing back again. Yes, tell Mr. Warren and let *him* decide whether to pursue the Truth. At least she would have done *something*. But tell him right at the end of the year, the last day of school, after everyone had left. That would give the whole summer to see what would happen before she started Continuation School in the fall.

The last day came and the Senior Fourths filed out of Room Six for the final time. Mr. Warren stood at the door and shook hands with each as he or she departed. Margy hung back so as to be the last out of the room and have Mr. Warren alone for a few moments. The Marker brothers shot past her, baseball and bats in hand, heading for the door and freedom. Orlie had not sat for the Entrances since he had known all along that his father expected him to help on the farm full-time now that he had finished Senior Fourth.

The teacher shook Margy's hand solemnly and moved as if to close the door after her. "It looks like you're the last of all," he said. It suddenly occurred to Margy that, after a month of silliness and pranks from the class, Mr. Warren might be as eager for the end of the year as his scholars.

Margy smiled at him shyly. "Mr. Warren, sir . . . ,"
she began, and hesitated.

"Chin up, Margy," said the teacher, rather quietly.
"It's not easy being 'from away.' I've been in Bancroft
for fourteen and a half years now, and they still call me
'the new teacher.'"

Margy opened and closed her mouth twice. "Mr.
Warren," she began again.

The door which Mr. Warren had closed crashed
open right beside them, and two girls from Junior
Fourth galloped through, both speaking at once.

"Mr. Warren, there's a fight—"

"Sir, Cline Marker and Chauncy Allen are—"

"—with baseball bats!"

"—*blood and everything . . .*"

Mr. Warren muttered something very un-teacherish
under his breath and charged off after the two girls,
leaving Margy alone in the silence of Room Six. She
stood for a moment looking at the empty desks. Then
she slowly picked up her book bag, pushed her glasses
up on her nose, and trudged home to the Fine House.

The next day, being the Saturday after school was out,
was declared a holiday by Aunt Alice. Margy was
allowed to come straggling down the stairs at nine-
fifteen and enjoy a leisurely breakfast before beginning
her Saturday chores. Aunt Edith promised to make a
special celebratory treat for the club meeting after
lunch.

Margy's club, The Order of the White Cloud, had

begun meeting again most Saturdays in the old garage near the back door of the Fine House. Its four members, Margy and Lenore, Jane and Cora, had to share their clubhouse with the five chickens, nameless, the Aunts were keeping this summer, but neither members nor hens minded this arrangement since the fowl had their pen at one end of the garage and the club headquarters was a collection of used furniture at the other.

Sometimes the club held its meeting after the Saturday matinee at the movies. Then the main order of business was to discuss the plot of the movie and its stars, and maybe even act part of it out. Cora Parker was particularly good at the swashbuckling roles, and her twin sister and Lenore took turns being the leading lady. Margy filled in all the other characters and acted as director. Bing good-naturedly took the role of any animal necessary, be it dog, horse, or whatever.

Today, however, everyone arrived for the meeting a little bit late and Lenore didn't have enough money for the movie anyway, so they decided to lounge in the clubhouse and revel in their new-found freedom from school. They munched on Aunt Edith's special treat, brownies warm from the oven. Naturally conversation drifted to the end of school and plans for the summer, if not indeed, "Plans for the Rest of One's Life."

"Everybody say what they want to be when they finish Continuation School," instructed President Margy through a bite of brownie. (All four members had sat for the Entrances.) "Jane, you begin." This was to prevent the gentle Jane from being influenced by what the others said.

"I'm going to be a nurse," said Jane immediately and firmly. Even Cora looked surprised by her twin's lofty ambition. They all wondered how the squeamish Jane, who went into hysterics at the sight of her own blood, would survive an operating theatre. No one, however, pointed out this truth, and Cora proceeded with the survey.

"*I'm* going to be a movie star," she announced grandly. "Ride horses, jump out of burning buildings . . . kiss Clark Gable and Jimmy Stewart." She struck a pose. "You know how it is, dah-ling. You simply *must* come and visit me in Hollywood."

"We will," the other three said in chorus, and Lenore threw a cushion at Cora by way of an exclamation mark.

"Now, Lenore," instructed Margy. "What are you going to be? My guess is a teacher, probably Senior First or Junior Second age."

"No, not a teacher," said Lenore quickly. "Verna's the one who wants to be a teacher. But she'll probably just end up working in her Pa's fancy store, like all her sisters." Lenore stopped abruptly and looked at Margy. "Oh, Margy," she said in a stricken voice. It was an unwritten law of the Order of the White Cloud that no member make any reference to Verna or the Emporium or the missing money. The fact that Verna, a charter member of the Club, was not allowed to attend meetings was reminder enough.

Margy had not talked to Verna since the raw March day she had walked out to Orlie's farm. It was so hard to sit just across the classroom from her and not be able to talk to her. Several times after their encounter in front of the Emporium Verna had defied her father's edict and sent Margy notes by way of Lenore. But she had stopped that because, for Margy, getting the notes was somehow worse than not communicating at all, and besides it made Lenore feel guilty and afraid being the go-between. Her father was on the School Board with Mr. Cooper.

Margy simply brushed the reference to Verna aside. "It's okay, Lenore. Tell us about what you want to be."

Lenore considered for a moment, then said, "I don't know. I never really thought about it. I guess I'll just get married and have lots of kids." Being an only child, Lenore rather fancied a big family.

Cora nudged Margy and said in a loud stage whisper, "'Mrs. Snuffy Farrow and all the little Snuffies,'" and pitched the cushion back at Lenore, who blushed magnificently and then quickly redirected the club's attention.

"What about you, Margy. What are you going to be when you finish school? I'll bet you'll be a fancy secretary to some big-shot executive."

"No," said Margy. "Not with my spelling. Not a secretary. What I want to do is fix ladies' hair for them and make them all beautiful and stuff. . . ." She trailed off a little lamely because this was the first time she had said it out loud and she wasn't sure how the others would react.

But the others looked suitably impressed. Cora said generously, "That's swell, Margy. You can come to Hollywood with me and make me look beautiful." She tossed her thick brown braids contemptuously. "I wish Ma would let me get my hair bobbed. It's such a nuisance braiding it every morning. And I'm always losing my hair ribbons."

"And you're always losing *my* hair ribbons too," added the aggrieved Jane. "I sure wish you had short hair too. Then people would stop saying," (her voice went up to a mocking falsetto), " 'Oh, are they *twins?*' I get so tired of being 'half of the Parker Twins.' "

"Say, Margy," said the daring Cora, "Let's pretend that you're an elegant hair dresser and you cut my hair for me."

"Oh, Cora, I couldn't. What would your mother say?"

"She wouldn't mind a bit," said Cora airily. "Why, only this morning she said that if I didn't sit still while she tried to comb it, she'd chop it all off." (Her voice took on a hurt tone.) "She said that my hair is always full of rats' nests."

"I suppose it would be all right to pretend," said Margy hesitantly. Then, with a rising enthusiasm, "Wait here and I'll run home and get some stuff."

She slipped into the Fine House. Happily Aunt Alice was at the library and Aunt Edith was having a tea break on the front verandah. Margy helped herself to Aunt Alice's good shears from her sewing basket and borrowed a clutch of hairpins and the silver hand mirror from her Aunt's chiffonnier. She also collected a towel and comb from the bathroom and several old magazines from the parlour. She had seen enough movies to know what a real beauty parlour should look like.

In no time at all the clubhouse had been transformed into "Chez Marguerite," with a waiting area complete with two customers reading magazines and her first client, Jane, perched on the three-legged stool with the towel cape around her shoulders.

"Now, Madame, what would you like?" Margy

untied Jane's long braids and ran the comb through her dark silky hair. Jane only giggled in a most unhelpful way so Margy rebraided her hair and coiled the two long pigtails around Jane's small shapely head, securing the coronet with hair pins. The result was really quite satisfactory. Jane twisted her head, trying to get the full effect in the small mirror. Margy unpinned the cape in her most efficient manner and said, "Next?"

Lenore was next. She perched on the stool and Margy pinned the towel around her saying, in what she hoped approximated a French accent, "Madame needs to add some height to her petite stature. I shall give ze coiffure."

She gathered Lenore's fine hair up into a topknot on the back of her head. To be sure a few tendrils of the soft blond hair slipped out at the back but they all agreed that this merely added to the effect, and gave Lenore a plaintive, romantic look.

"Zat will be three dollars and twenty-five cents, Madame. Please pay the cashier on ze way out," said Margy, flushed with her success, and glad she had charged Lenore an outrageous amount for her hair style.

"Now me!" demanded Cora, plumping herself down on the stool and pulling the ribbons off the bottom of her dark braids.

Margy loosened the pigtails and ran the comb through the long rippling hair. (Mrs. Parker's comments about "rats' nests" notwithstanding, Margy encountered only one small tangle.) She snipped the scissors through the air near Cora's head, pretending to cut the hair.

"Oh, go ahead," said Cora recklessly. "Just trim it a bit. Nobody will even notice."

Margy cut the least little sliver off the bottom. The scissors felt thoroughly satisfying cutting through Cora's thick hair. Cora examined the results in the mirror.

"That looks good, but take more off, Margy." She made a chopping motion just below her ear with her hand. "Right there. I want the Greta Garbo look."

Like a person hypnotized, Margy made a deep cut. Lenore and Jane watched, their jaws slack, their eyes round with horror. Margy continued her careful line across the back of Cora's neck. The sharp scissors cut smoothly through the thick hair and it fell in clumps to the towel and the floor below. Margy felt totally in control, with power over the scissors, Cora's appearance, and the whole situation. She bit her lip and furrowed her brow in deep concentration.

The irrepressible Cora: "Now bangs. I want bangs. Kind of slinky, over to the side."

Margy combed a section to the front and cut it carefully, then recombed and tidied the stray ends. Cora peered into the hand mirror and nodded with emphatic satisfaction.

"Now, that's more like it," she said approvingly. "Light and cool and . . . businesslike. And no more tangles."

Jane found her voice. It was faint and far away but tinged with astonished admiration. "That looks really *good,* Margy. How'd you learn to do that?"

Margy shook her head. "I don't know. I could just see inside my head what it should look like and then I did it with the scissors."

Then of course the other three wanted to try it too, so Margy sat down on the stool. "Now just a little bit," she said. She was trying to grow her hair long and even the smallest trim would be a setback. So it was decided: Jane would cut the left side, Lenore the right, and Cora the back and the bangs so they could all have a go at it. Margy was not at all sure she liked this idea but these were her only three friends in the whole wide world, and they had let her do their hair, so she had to be a good sport.

Jane first. She trimmed neatly across the bottom below Margy's left ear, cutting less than a quarter inch of hair away. Margy checked the mirror and allowed herself a relieved sigh. Lenore matched her clip for clip on the other side, although she pointedly complained that the left-handed person in the group (meaning Cora) would have found it easier.

Cora took the long scissors from Lenore and circled Margy before she attacked the rear. Margy was grateful that the boisterous Cora was not snipping around her ears, but she wished she had a magic mirror that would allow her to see what was going on back there. She held her breath while Cora scissored enthusiastically and confidently.

"There," said Cora with finality. "Perfect."

"No it's not," countered Jane. "It's higher here than it is there."

"That," Cora explained patiently, "is because you two didn't make it even at the front."

"It looks even at the front to me," said Margy nervously, peering into the mirror.

"Well, it isn't," said Cora with certainty. "I'll just

trim it a bit over there."

Snip went the scissors. And snip again.

"Now it's definitely longer on my side," Jane pointed out with the satisfaction of one who has been proven right. Cora came around and considered it.

"Yes," she had to concede. "It is a bit longer here. That's what comes of having three different people doing the cutting. The best thing to do now is just let me trim the whole thing off evenly."

"But . . . ," said Margy. She was quite sure that was not the Best Thing to do.

"Now, just you sit still and don't worry." Cora attacked the problem with knit-brow determination. The other two girls subsided into silence on the old couch. Bing, who had been asleep in the crack of sunlight near the door, opened one eye and returned Margy's wild-eyed stare with mild interest.

By the time Cora was sure that all sides of Margy's hair were sufficiently even, her hair was *very* short.

The other three assured her that the effect was just fine. Lenore pronounced it "swell," and Jane said kindly that she looked "quite chic" and in fact a good deal like Gloria Swanson, the movie star.

The meeting of the Order of the White Cloud broke up quite rapidly, however, after that. The other three members melted into the lengthening afternoon shadows and Margy slowly tidied up the clubhouse by herself and fed the chickens. Then she collected the scissors and towel, Aunt Edith's plate and Bing, and headed with dragging feet towards the Fine House.

The Aunts were in the kitchen preparing supper when Margy appeared at the back door.

Aunt Alice said, "Mercy!"

Aunt Edith said, "Oh, my *Lord!*"

"What happened?" said Aunt Alice.

"We were playing Hairdresser and Cora . . . ." Margy's voice sounded far-away in her own ears. Then, "Oh, Auntalice, does it look terrible?"

"It looks," said Aunt Alice, "as if someone turned a pudding bowl upside down on your head and cut all around the edges with a pair of dull pinking shears. I thought you were trying to let your hair grow longer."

There was a sharp rap at the front door. Margy fled upstairs out of sight before Aunt Alice could answer it. She went into the bathroom and peered into the big mirror over the sink. Tears began to run slowly down her cheeks. She ran across the hall into her own little room, threw herself down on her bed and curled up into a tight ball of sobbing misery. I'll never go outside again, she vowed, until it all grows back in.

She heard the bedroom door nudge open. Bing pressed his wet nose up against her arm. Margy was too miserable even to accept his doggy sympathy. A minute or two later she heard Aunt Alice's slow laboured step on the stairs. Bing oozed under the bed and pulled his rope tail in after himself out of sight.

Aunt Alice came through the doorway and snapped on the light. "That," she said, "was Mrs. Parker and her twins at the door. That is, they *used* to be twins. In any case, she is not all that happy with what you did to Cora's hair." Aunt Alice pursed her lips. "I told her that I wasn't that thrilled with what Cora did to your hair either."

Aunt Alice's gentle hand smoothed Margy's tousled

cropped hair and she ran her finger down her wet cheek. "You ask me, Cora got the better of the deal. And I thought what you did to Jane's hair was right smart. Made her look really aristocratic. However," Aunt Alice's voice became severe again, "that doesn't excuse the fact that you shouldn't have cut Cora's hair without asking Mrs. Parker first. And you shouldn't have let those girls cut your hair either. You'll have to learn not to get carried away with the moment so easily, Margy, and to stand up for yourself."

"Yes, Auntalice."

"Therefore, I'm 'gating' you for two full weeks. You will not be allowed to go outside the yard for fourteen days—except to church, of course—not down street, not to the library, not visiting, not anything."

"Yes, Auntalice." A hope crossed Margy's mind. "Maybe you shouldn't let me go to church either, Auntalice. After all, gated is gated." Ralph Phillips and his mother went to St. John's Church every Sunday.

"Not go to church?" Aunt Alice raised her considerable eyebrows. Margy may as well have said, "Not eat," or "Not breathe."

"But Ral . . . everyone will stare at me," Margy's voice raised in a wail.

"I will tie your hair, what's left of it, up in rags after you have your bath on Saturday night and it will come out all curly. And I'll trim it into a smart 'Buster Brown' cut. I saw a picture in the last *Ladies' Home Journal.*"

Buster Brown sounded a long way from Gloria Swanson. "I'm never going outside again," said Margy to her Aunt's retreating back.

"'Never' is a long time, Margy," Aunt Alice called back. "Now get cleaned up and come down for supper. And for heaven's sake, bring that dog down with you. You know he's not supposed to be upstairs."

"Never is a long time," Aunt Alice had said. Why, just two weeks is forever when one is "gated" during a beautiful July in Bancroft. The worst part was that it meant Margy couldn't go down street on Thursday to pick up a *Bancroft Times*. The Aunts knew the Entrance Examination results would most likely be printed in the next edition of the *Times*. If only Margy could see it before they did. She felt that she had done all right in the Entrances, but she fervently hoped that she had done well. That might atone somewhat for the cloud over her school year.

Aunt Alice picked up a paper on her way home from the library towards the end of Margy's second week of gating. Margy, polishing silver in the kitchen with Lenore who had come over for the afternoon, could see it sticking out the top of her book bag. She would have loved to run over and quickly scan the pages to see if the results were printed yet, but she knew that would just not do, so she kept polishing the same spoon over and over and watched the Aunts. She and Lenore exchanged an apprehensive look.

The two Aunts settled on either side of the kitchen table (as usual) and Aunt Edith shook out the paper with studied concentration, without so much as a glance at the two girls. She lingered over the first page (as usual) reading tidbits of interest, beginning with the death notices (as usual). Everyone in the village knew who had died over the past week, but they still read the notices to enjoy the elegant and dignified descriptions of their hitherto quite ordinary neighbours.

Aunt Edith read, "'Mr. R.A. Campbell received a wire Tuesday evening informing him that the Angel of Death had visited his father. He left immediately by motor to attend the obsequies.'"

"Last week," interjected Aunt Alice, "they said 'Angle of Death.' At least they got it right this time."

"Now, look at this," continued Aunt Edith placidly. "It describes the Macleod wedding as 'a quiet affair.'" She read: "'The bride was becomingly attired in navy blue crepe with black shoes and hat to match.'"

"Would you like me to read the next instalment of 'Murder on the Bridge' to you while you drink your tea, Alice?"

Aunt Edith took a slow sip of tea and carefully turned the page, scanning it for the next chapter of the continuing serial. Then, in mild surprise, "Well, would you look at this. The results of the Entrance Examinations are printed already." (Margy stopped polishing the spoon, closed her eyes, and held her breath.)

Aunt Edith looked down the list. Margy could hear the smile in her voice. "And here's our Margy, with honours, second in the whole class."

Margy let out her breath, opened her eyes, dropped the silver spoon on the floor, and hugged Lenore.

"And here's Lenore, too," continued Aunt Edith. She kindly did not add where Lenore's name came on the list, but the placid Lenore didn't seem to care all that much, so long as it appeared somewhere above the pass line.

"That's very good, dear," said Aunt Alice gravely, peering across the table at the page Aunt Edith held up. "Although they have you printed as 'Margery Stratton' in the list. The only person to beat you was Bedelia Summerson." There were dozens of Summersons in Bancroft, and they always came first in their classes.

Lenore still had her short arms around Margy's waist, grinning proudly at her friend. "Don't you never mind, Margy," she said happily, "My pa says that 'hell is so full of Summersons that their feet is sticking out the windows.'"

"*Lenore!*" said both Aunts together in one shocked voice. But Margy laughed and hugged the sympathetic Lenore all the more.

"We do not say that word in this house, Lenore," said Aunt Alice primly. "Please remember that. If you must use an expression like that, kindly substitute the word 'Haliburton.'" Margy thought it was even funnier to picture Summerson feet sticking out of the windows of Haliburton.

Aunt Alice relented and smiled at the two girls before her. "Well, it looks as if you're both honest-to-goodness high school scholars now. Margy, you must write to your father tonight and tell him how well you did. I expect that you will be the very first Stratton to get a high school education." She said that with great satisfaction, as if Margy weren't also the first Mullett to go to Continuation School as well.

"Yes, Auntalice."

"And . . . I guess it's about time to lift the gating.

Your two weeks would be up on Saturday anyway. Would you girls like to trot down and pick up the mail?"

"*Yes,* Auntalice!"

Margy and Lenore pranced off down Flint Street on feet with wings. Margy's vow to never again be seen in public was forgotten. Her Buster Brown haircut shone in the late afternoon sun, and the clipping from the *Times* was tucked, like a good luck talisman, deep in her skirt pocket.

Margy was relieved that she had not only passed, but done well. And she was delighted that Aunt Alice was pleased. Aunt Alice who said, "Who cares what the outside world thinks," but who nonetheless had to maintain the Mullett name in the community.

Margy was glad she had done well for the Aunts. And for Daddy. And for Mr. Warren. As for the rest of the Senior Fourths, well, she had beat almost the whole lot of them.

So there.

CHAPTER
8

"Oh, please, Auntalice. Please, please, please, PUL-LEEZE!" Margy's voice took on its most beseeching tone.

Aunt Alice looked at Margy, then at Mr. Strong, then back at Margy.

Mr. Strong twisted his cap in his hands. "You think about it, Miss Mullett," he said, "and let The Management know." (Mr. Strong always referred to his wife as "The Management.") "I'll be back in town on Wednesday and I could pick Margy up then." He backed out of the kitchen door and turned towards his truck, settling his battered cap on his head as he walked away.

Margy turned pleading eyes to Aunt Alice again. Here was her chance to earn the money for the Wonderful Gift. The year was more than half over and her fund was discouraging low, only one dollar and twelve cents. (The Wonderful Gift had been preying on Margy's mind all week, ever since Lenore, who was in on the secret, had checked the Emporium again last Saturday to make sure the blue dressing gown was still there. Thankfully it was, and Lenore had craftily moved it to an out-of-the-way rack.)

Moreover, a chance to get away from Bancroft for the summer, away from the shadow of the Lonely Time, would be wonderful. Then she could be just plain "Margy Stratton from Bancroft," instead of "Margy Stratton, that girl who probably took the poor peoples' money at Christmas." On her own she could prove to herself that she could be smart and independent like Aunt Alice, and come back rich into the bargain.

And, of course, what fun to have a job at an elegant guest house in the country, to see new places and meet fascinating new people. Margy had never been to Fort Stewart, but she had heard Mrs. Strong talk about it endlessly during her stays at the Fine House.

Mrs. Strong was the very same Mrs.-Strong-from-Fort-Stewart who came every spring to sew for the Aunts. In one week her shirring machine could turn out whatever shirtwaists, dresses, nighties, and "step-ins" were needed by the household, as well as curtains, tablecloths and napkins. From scraps and remnants she created aprons, tea cosies and pot holders for the church bazaar.

Creative? My, yes. And musical. If she heard a song once on the radio she could play it back on the old piano in the parlour. And a great cook, too. Aunt Edith always worked extra hard on her bread and pies all the week Mrs. Strong was around, just so as not to lose face.

But mostly what Margy admired about Mrs. Strong was her precision and efficiency. Mrs. Strong could sew a seam by hand so fine that it looked as though it had been sewn on Aunt Alice's pedal Singer sewing machine.

All of these qualities made Mrs. Strong perfect for what she did in the summer, when she wasn't in demand as a seamstress, and that was manage a guest house in her home in Fort Stewart. Margy was terribly sorry to hear that Mrs. Strong had hurt her leg, especially now at the beginning of the summer, just as her guests were about to arrive. But as Aunt Alice said, "It's an ill wind that blows nobody good," and in this case the very same wind that broke the branch that shied the horse that tipped the wagon that hurt Mrs. Strong's leg . . . seemed to be blowing a wonderful opportunity for independence and earning money in Margy's direction.

Mr. Strong had stopped in to inquire (in as few words as possible, as was his way) whether Margy would be interested in spending the summer at Fort Stewart helping Mrs. Strong with her "paying guests."

Interested? Margy could scarcely contain herself as Mr. Strong climbed into his battered truck and started jerkily off down the hill towards Cow Bell Alley. Her mind was whirling. Two dollars and fifty cents a week, Mr. Strong had said, plus room and board. Two dollars and fifty cents a week for four weeks was ten *whole dollars*.

Aunt Alice looked hesitant. This was a good sign. When Aunt Alice looked determined one knew her mind was already made up and there was no use teasing to get her to change her it. But if she looked doubtful there was a chance.

"I suppose we could manage in the garden without her," she said slowly.

"And the summer in the country would be pleasant,"

added Aunt Edith. She didn't like the hot sticky weather of July and early August.

"Now mind that Mrs. Strong will expect you to work hard and do a good job, Margy," said Aunt Alice. "There can be no fooling around. That woman has absolutely no sense of humour."

"Yes, Auntalice," said Margy promptly, knowing the battle was won. In her inner soul she was thinking of the long cool summer evenings in the elegant guest house, the opportunities to go swimming in the lake in the afternoons, the sumptuous meals that Mrs. Strong was sure to prepare and . . . well, yes, the ten dollars.

As soon as the telephone operator was back on duty after her lunch, Aunt Alice had her ring through to Boulter and get Mrs. Strong on the line. Aunt Alice always shouted into the telephone when it was a long-distance call, as if she were required to make her voice carry that extra twenty miles.

"Yes, Mrs. Strong, my NIECE will be GLAD to come out and give you a HAND this SUMMER. Of course, you NEEDN'T pay her; she's happy to HELP YOU OUT."

(You needn't *what*, thought Margy in the background, but apparently Mrs. Strong was a businesswoman and overrode Aunt Alice's generosity.)

"Well, WHATEVER you say Mrs. Strong. I know she'll WORK HARD for you." Aunt Alice rang off the line. "Mr. Strong will pick you up on Wednesday about noon, Margy, when he comes to town to get some more supplies."

Margy had two days to get ready. Aunt Edith loaned her an old carpet bag for her things. Margy packed three cotton dresses, several aprons, her bathing costume, and her money box to keep her earnings in. She also included several favourite books to read if she got bored, and some stamped envelopes so she could write to Daddy. (And write to Aunt Alice and tell her she had arrived safely. Aunt Alice said that the telephone, especially long distance, was only for emergencies or to pass on urgent messages.)

Mr. Strong picked Margy up just after lunch on Wednesday. He wedged her little carpet bag in among the bags of sugar and flour and other supplies in the truck, and they were off. Aunt Alice and Aunt Edith stood at the front gate and waved them down the hill and around the corner. Bing sat beside them, Aunt Alice holding his collar as he waved his rope tail sadly.

It was a long ride to Fort Stewart. The shy Mr. Strong was a taciturn Scot if ever there was one, and answered Margy's stream of questions in a monosyllable, or sometimes with merely a nod of his shaggy head. By the time they neared "the Fort," the only information that Margy had gleaned was that there were already several guests at the house, that The Management was getting around some better on her sore leg, and that there would be fresh rhubarb cobbler for supper (evidently a favourite of Mr. Strong's since this was the only item of information that he actually volunteered).

The rolling hills of the countryside were magnificent as they drove steadily northward. Finally the farms got closer together and they passed a school and a tiny general store at a crossroads.

"Be sure you tell me when we're getting close to Fort Stewart," said Margy anxiously to Mr. Strong.

Mr. Strong turned and gave Margy a long stare. "We

just *came through* Fort Stewart," he said solemnly.

Less than a mile later he turned in a long dusty lane and pulled up behind a rambling farmhouse. "Here we are," he said.

Here we are where, thought Margy. Where was the gracious guest house, the sweeping lawns, the *piazza* where the guests could linger over coffee in the evening?

Clutching her carpet bag, Margy cautiously stepped across the back porch and into the kitchen. Mrs. Strong was sitting at the table with her leg propped up on another chair. She was shelling peas into a large yellow bowl.

"Oh, Margy," she said heartily, "There you are. I'm so glad you decided to come. Now you run upstairs and put your bag in your room—last door on your left at the top of the back stairs—and then get right back down here and I'll put you to work. You're going to have to be my feet for the next few weeks."

Margy found her room, grabbed an apron out of her bag, and was downstairs in a flash. Within the next hour she had dug potatoes from the garden, washed and scraped them, refilled the woodbox and fed the fire in the big stove in the summer kitchen, basted the roast twice, picked and chopped the rhubarb for the cobbler, and carried in two pails of water from the pump.

During supper she was kept busy running back and forth to the kitchen refilling bowls and clearing dishes away. Mrs. Strong explained to her guests that Margy was there to be her helper and do her running for the rest of the summer. The guests smiled their approval at Margy and henceforth called her "Feet." Margy wasn't upset since she knew the name didn't refer to the size of her feet, but to their ability and mobility.

When the guests—there were four of them, two older couples—retired to the front porch, Margy got to eat her own supper in the kitchen. Never had a meal tasted so delicious. (Aunt Alice said that "hunger is a savoury sauce," and that was certainly true tonight.) Mrs. Strong kept saying things like, "Might as well finish off them peas; we can have fresh tomorrow," and "You just scrape out that cream jug onto your cobbler there."

As Margy washed the supper dishes, Mrs. Strong sat at the kitchen table and instructed her on where to put dishes and utensils away in their exact correct position. She also described the morning routine.

"Do you have an alarm clock, Margy?"

"No, ma'am." Margy hadn't known she'd need one so her little "Baby Ben" clock was still sitting safely at home on her bedside table.

"Don't worry about it, I have one I can loan you," said Mrs. Strong comfortably. "You had better set it for five because there's a good deal to get ready by breakfast time."

Margy nodded attentively.

Mrs. Strong continued, "Breakfast will be porridge— the oatmeal is in that bin there, and we'll put it to soak tonight—and eggs-over-easy and bacon—cut it good and thick, mind—and sliced tomatoes. You can pick them fresh off the vine tomorrow morning and sprinkle them with onions and parsley. Oh yes, and put the brown sugar on the table. One of the guests likes brown sugar on his tomatoes. We'll make lots of coffee and while they're eating the porridge you can start making the toast. The toasting fork hangs on a nail behind the stove and you can rake out a good bed of coals in the stove when you're ready to start."

What a breakfast, thought Margy. At home the first meal of the day was probably a warm muffin, a glass of milk and an apple. Well, maybe on a bitterly cold winter morning Aunt Edith would make a pot of oatmeal porridge "to stick to their ribs" until noon. But here in Fort Stewart, porridge seemed to be standard fare even in the middle of summer.

Margy set her borrowed alarm clock to ring at four forty-five just to be on the safe side, but then kept waking up every half hour or so, afraid that she had somehow missed it and overslept. When the shrill bell aroused her she jumped out of bed. It was time to start earning that ten dollars. Margy kept the image of the blue dressing gown firmly in her mind as she pulled her clothes on in the chill morning dark. Creeping down the creaky back stairs, she entered the kitchen with her plan of attack in place. (Two tiny house mice scurried out of her determined way as she crossed the kitchen floor and lit the lamp.)

Lay the fire. Light the fire. Fill the woodbox. Salt and stir the porridge and put it on the back of the stove. Lay the table in the big dining room, starting with a clean tablecloth and napkins from the sideboard where Mrs. Strong had told her to find them. Turn the dampers on the stove to hold the fire. Stir the porridge. Fetch the tomatoes, wash and slice them onto a platter. (Don't forget the brown sugar.) Feed the fire. Grind the coffee. Fill the jam pots from the icebox: strawberry jam, raspberry jam, apple butter, honey, maple syrup. Set out the butter to allow it to get soft. Stir the porridge again; add water to thin it down. Slice the bacon ("nice and thick"). Count the eggs out in a bowl.

By the time Mrs. Strong came hobbling down the stairs at quarter to seven, Margy was hot and tired but triumphant in her domain.

"Well, you done real fine," said Mrs. Strong, observing the order about her. She took over the bacon and egg production. It was a matter of pride with her that the eggs for her guests were cooked to perfection: solid white, runny centre, and turned ever so gently so that not one yolk broke open.

After the guests had been fed and the dishes done, there was much work to do: straightening and tidying their rooms came first. Margy refilled the big washing pitchers in each room after carrying out the used water standing in the wash bowls beside them. She had to step carefully so as not to spill on the carpet going down the stairs. It was an unpleasant job, emptying the cold slimy water with soap scum and whiskers floating on top. After that an even more unpleasant job: emptying the chamber pots (Mr. Strong called them "Thunder Mugs") from under each bed. Margy tried to remember why she had wanted this job so badly. She closed her eyes and thought of Aunt Alice's Wonderful Gift.

Next the eggs had to be collected from the henhouse and following that came the ironing. Mrs. Strong was most particular that the linen tablecloth and napkins be perfectly smooth and crisp. By the time that was done there was lunch to prepare, and then the huge garden to weed, baking to do, bread to set, and supper to start. Mrs. Strong did a creditable job, carrying on as many tasks as she could from a sitting position, but by eight-thirty that evening Margy was so tired that she wondered if she would be able to crawl up the stairs to her room. She fell asleep with her clothes on and it seemed only minutes later that the insistent ringing of her alarm clock was calling her back to the reality that another twenty-seven days stretched out in front of her. She tried to think of the beautiful blue dressing gown for inspiration, but she was so tired she could scarcely remember what it looked like.

Friday was the day to do end-of-the-week laundry so that was begun promptly after breakfast. Once it was pegged firmly to the line behind the farmhouse, Mrs. Strong instructed Margy to use the hot soapy water that was left in the tub to wash the kitchen floor and out onto the back porch.

"You do that, dearie, and I'll start on lunch," she said.

Her husband stuck his head in the back door. "Feet, did you pick up the eggs yet this morning? Them hens is clucking something fierce."

"Feet" had to admit that she had forgotten, but Mrs. Strong allowed as how she herself would enjoy the short walk to the henhouse and that she would get the eggs.

Margy scrubbed and mopped the kitchen floor, backing out the door and across the porch. She even moved the old bench over and carefully mopped under it. Mr. Strong appeared to help her tote the heavy tub of wash water around the corner of the house and dump it. Margy decided that, although he was very quiet and solemn, he was on the whole a kind person. He had helped her out several times when the job was simply too heavy for her to handle.

The two returned just in time to see Mrs. Strong limp back up the porch steps, holding the corners of her apron as a bag for the eggs she had collected. With the other hand she managed her cane and stepped carefully over the wet spots on the porch to avoid slipping. She paused and rested her ample posterior on the small bench just outside the door before proceeding.

Alas! When Margy had moved the bench to wash underneath it she had not returned it to its proper position, and as Mrs. Strong rested her heavy girth against it, the bench shifted to the left and one leg of it slipped off the edge of the porch. Mrs. Strong let out a screech that ranged through two full octaves and could be heard by small animals as far away as New Carlow. In the blink of an eye she was sitting on the sopping floor with a lap full of smashed eggs.

Margy couldn't help it. Maybe it was just plain tiredness, or nervousness, or simply the comical aspect of the plump Mrs. Strong sitting there surrounded by fragments of eggshell and sticky mess. But Margy started to giggle. The more she tried to stop the worse it got. Even the taciturn Mr. Strong, once he was sure that his wife hadn't hurt her other leg, threw back his shaggy head and began to laugh, a deep hearty laugh that started in his boots and worked its way steadily upwards until it exploded from the midst of his beard. Margy had never heard it before.

When Margy and Mr. Strong were finally breathless

from laughter, Mrs. Strong, who had collected her scattered dignity and struggled to her feet, said grimly, "I'm glad you two can glean so much enjoyment from this. You," (she glared at Margy), "can get some water and clean up this mess . . . and you," (now a glare for Mr. Strong who had once more retreated into his quiet shell), "you I want to see in the house." She turned, humped through the door, and was gone.

Mr. Strong laid his finger sadly beside his nose and looked at Margy. "Oh, Feet," he said, "It looks like we're in trouble with The Management now."

The next morning after breakfast Mrs. Strong told Margy that Mr. Strong was going into town that day for the last load of supplies, and Margy was to go with him. This batch of guests was leaving that day anyway, and besides, Mrs. Strong had been in touch by 'phone with a niece in Boulter who would be taking the job. She was older than Margy, and stronger. And besides she was family.

On the return trip to town, Mr. Strong was much more chatty, pointing out various leaves and flowers, and telling Margy who lived on what farm. Margy was the silent one; indeed, she was so tired she could scarcely keep from falling asleep up against Mr. Strong's shoulder. Besides she was most discouraged about ever earning enough money to buy Aunt Alice's Wonderful Gift. As the wheels of the little truck bumped along the road they set up a rhythmic drubbing: *a dollar, twelve cents; a dollar, twelve cents.* Margy's head drooped sadly towards her chest.

The next time she looked up they were pulling up in front of the Fine House. Mr. Strong dug in his trousers pocket and then tried to press five quarters into Margy's hand.

"But I didn't work for even half a week," protested Margy weakly.

"No, you take it all right, Feet," said Mr. Strong. "It was sure worth it to me."

Margy thought the Aunts might be upset at her rapid return from the world of commerce. But they were delighted to have her back home. Aunt Edith went so far as to say it had been "real lonely without her around," and Bing near to wagged his tail off.

The Aunts made her relate every single detail of her adventure, including the scene of Mrs. Strong and the Scrambled Eggs, several times. Margy showed them the five quarters Mr. Strong had given her at the front gate. "Do you think it was all right to take the money?" she said anxiously. "Mr. Strong said it was worth it to him. . . ."

Aunt Alice nodded. "Yes," she said serenely, "I'm sure he doesn't get too much to laugh about. Even I would pay at least a dollar and a quarter to enjoy that spectacle."

Margy curled her fingers around the money. Now she had two dollars and thirty-seven cents. But *such* a long way to go.

CHAPTER
9

The hot late-July sun shone mercilessly down on the vegetable patch where Margy and Aunt Alice were picking yellow beans from the long rows.

"Why don't people plant gardens in the shade?" said Margy crossly. "It would be much more pleasant to pick if we were in the shade."

"Because of course, dear, plants need sunshine to grow," replied Aunt Alice quite unnecessarily and without the slightest hint of sarcasm.

Does she really think I don't know that, thought Margy darkly. I should have asked why we don't grow the darn beans in the winter when they would stay frozen instead of having to "put them up" in preserving jars.

"When we finish these two rows we shall stop for lunch," Aunt Alice decreed, straightening her back. "Your Aunt Edith should be calling us in for lunch any minute."

Margy's long skinny fingers flew through the dark leaves like a machine, stripping the thick waxy beans from the plants. She finished her row first and then helped Aunt Alice complete hers.

But Aunt Edith was not quite ready for lunch when they appeared at the back door carrying the basket. Margy was afraid that Aunt Alice would put her to work snapping the ends off and slicing the beans to ready them for preserving, definitely Aunt Edith's department. But instead she said, "Margy, how would you like to scamper down and see if the mail is in and sorted yet?"

How would she like? In no time at all Margy had washed her face and hands, combed her very short hair, and "scampered."

There was only one item of mail: a small thick cream-coloured envelope. There was no return address on the back, but it was postmarked Madoc, Ontario, which Margy knew was their next-door-neighbour village, about fifty miles south of Bancroft down the Hastings Road.

A letter from "Out Front"! (Well, almost Out Front.) And best of all, the spidery script on the envelope directed it to

Miss E. Marguerite Stratton,
In the care of Miss Alice Mullett,
Bancroft, Ontario
(County of Hastings) Canada

A letter for her very own self, and not even from Daddy. Margy would have loved to rip it open right then and there on the steps of the Post Office, but she knew that Aunt Alice would not look kindly upon such a display of impatience. Opening the post was a kind of ritual in the Fine House, an occasion to be anticipated and savoured. Margy tucked her mysterious letter into her pocket and headed for home.

Thankfully lunch was on the table when Margy got back to the Fine House. She propped her letter up against the sugar bowl in the centre of the table and laid Grandfather's silver letter opener beside it. Aunt Edith commented on the stamp. Then the Aunts discussed at length whom the sender might be. It would appear that they knew several families in Madoc, some of whom were distantly related to them on their Papa's side of the family.

Finally, when Margy thought she was going to burst, Aunt Alice said, "Aren't you going to open your letter, dear?" as if she were faintly surprised that Margy hadn't done so already.

Margy swooped up the letter and slit it open. The letter read:

July 22, 1933

My dear Marguerite,

Your cousin Annie and I were wondering if you might like to come to "Blue Willows" to visit us for a spell this summer. We are most anxious to get to know you out of our fondness for your dear late Mother. Our mutual cousin, Mr. Percy William Constant, will be driving from Bancroft to Belleville on August first, and would be able to drop you off on his way through and take you back a few days later. Hoping for a favourable reply,

Affectionately,
Your cousin,
Agnes Tummelty (Miss)

P. S. Do give my love to your dear Aunties.

Margy was enchanted with her letter. "Who is Miss Tummelty?" she asked.

"She is sort of a third or fourth cousin of ours, I think," replied Aunt Alice. "That makes her a third or fourth cousin 'once removed' to you. She and her sister live in their old family home in Madoc. An odd pair of ducks, if you ask me. They're in their sixties but people still call them 'The Girls.'"

Nobody had asked her so Margy didn't mention that some people in Bancroft called Aunt Alice and Aunt Edith "The Girls" behind their backs, and thought of them as a pair of odd ducks too, no doubt. Instead she asked, "May I go, Auntalice?"

Several weeks had gone by since her abortive attempt at independence, and Margy felt well over that episode. She was more than ready to try her wings again. Madoc was much farther away than Fort Stewart. There could be no rapid return from there. This time Margy would prove to herself and the Aunts that she could make it successfully in the outside world, on her own and by herself, with the shadow of the Lonely Time left far behind in Bancroft.

Aunt Alice looked at Aunt Edith. Aunt Edith looked at Aunt Alice. "I guess we could manage for a few days without her," said Aunt Alice reluctantly.

"They did think a lot of Lizzy," said Aunt Edith. (Margy loved it when they called her mother by her childhood name; everyone else referred to her as Elizabeth, and that was the name carved on her gravestone. Calling her Lizzy made it seem like she was right there.)

It was the "Lizzy" that carried the day. Aunt Alice

nodded. Aunt Edith nodded. Bing thumped his tail. Margy clapped her hands together gleefully.

"Now, you must get organized for your trip and 'pack your turkey,'" said Aunt Alice. "I'll help you."

"My what?" asked Margy, mystified. Did she have to bring food with her?

"Well, your bag, of course. Your valise, your grip." Aunt Alice was already making mental lists.

Apparently "packing one's turkey" to visit the Tummelty family home in Madoc carried more significance than just throwing some clothing into an old carpet bag to go to work in Fort Stewart. Margy was to have use of Aunt Alice's small leather suitcase, the one she had bought from the Eaton's catalogue to take to the Librarians' Convention in Hamilton several years earlier. Only Margy's best things were packed in it, including her good yellow organdy dress which Aunt Edith ironed "within an inch of its life" and folded with tissue paper to keep it nice, and for which Aunt Alice bought a silky new ribbon sash.

"I don't know what goes on in Madoc," said Aunt Alice firmly, "but it's best to be prepared in case you need to dress nicely. When we were young they used to have magnificent house parties in the Tummelty's lovely home. In any case you can wear it to church."

The following week Margy saved her Saturday night bath until Monday, the night before she was to leave. Aunt Alice helped her wash her hair (which had grown nearly half an inch in the month since the great hair-cutting escapade) and tied it up in strips of rags into many knobbly bunches so it would be curly the next day. It was rather hard to sleep on but Aunt Alice said, "First impressions are lasting impressions," so Margy could put up with a little discomfort to be as beautiful as possible when the Tummeltys first saw her.

"Why is their house called 'Blue Willows'?" Margy asked Aunt Alice as she was winding her hair.

"I'm not sure but I expect it's because they think it looks like the house on the Blue Willow plate pattern," said Aunt Alice.

On her way to bed Margy got the Blue Willow platter out of the sideboard in the dining room and examined it. Yes, there was a house, right at the bottom. Very Impressive. It seemed as if Margy were going to a very elegant place.

Cousin Percy William Constant drove up to the door in his "flivver" promptly at nine o'clock the next morning and held open the door for Margy. She waved gaily to the Aunts and Bing and they were off.

It was a bright and perfect summer day. Tuesday, the first day of August in the year of our Lord, one thousand, nine hundred and thirty-three. Who knew what significant events were happening Out Front in Belleville that very day, or even halfway Out Front in little Madoc. And she, Margy Stratton, would be part of it because she had remembered to say "Rabbits!" first thing this morning to give herself good luck all month. She did feel very lucky. Who cared if the hot dusty breeze through the windows of the ancient flivver was taking every bit of curl out of her special hair-do? She was off on an adventure!

Percy William was quite affable and had a story about every bend in the road, every lake, every settlement they passed through. He answered in detail all the questions Margy peppered him with. It was a long drive down the winding Hastings Road, and by the time they passed through Bannockburn, even Margy had run out of questions. They drove in companionable silence for a while and then Margy decided to share some of her knowledge with Percy William.

"Cousin Percy William," she said—she had already found out that everyone called him Percy William to distinguish him from his brother William Percy— "Cousin Percy William, do you know why the Tummeltys call their house 'Blue Willows'?"

Percy William shrugged affably. "It's because of a couple of old willow trees in the back garden, I guess. In a certain light, about dusk, they look kinda bluish, don't you know?"

Margy pondered this for a few miles. Percy William's explanation sounded plausible, but she hated the idea of Aunt Alice being wrong about anything. She considered asking Percy William about the appearance of the house, but decided to wait until she could see it for herself.

Soon they were in Madoc, passing down the high street. In Margy's opinion, this village wasn't nearly so pleasant or exciting as Bancroft, but then she had never actually lived here so she couldn't be absolutely sure.

They turned up a street of brick houses. In Bancroft, the fine houses were sprinkled throughout the town, rather like raisins in a rice pudding, but here in Madoc they all seemed to be clumped together in one spot like the icing on a cupcake.

Then she saw it, a large powerful brick house with

a white verandah crouching along three sides, high gables along the second storey, and a candle-snuffer tower at the left corner of the roof. Colourful flowers bloomed along the walkways, and at the edge of the front garden was a graceful willow tree.

But if the big house was "Blue Willows," why were four gangly boys playing baseball in the side yard, and why was Percy William pulling the flivver up in front of the much smaller, much shabbier house across the street from it?

Two ancient plump ladies came toddling out of the small house and made a tremendous fuss over Percy William, who had to bend down so they could kiss him. Margy had to bend down to be kissed as well, but it felt nice to be enveloped in two hugs at once, one smelling of gingerbread and the other of lilac water.

"Doesn't she look like her mother, Aggie?" said Cousin Annie, peering over her tiny glasses.

"Yes, the very image of Elizabeth," agreed Cousin Agnes, peering over *her* tiny glasses. Margy loved to hear this comment, although she knew it was polite fiction on their part; everyone else observed how she favoured Daddy's side of the family.

The two plump ladies led the way into their little house and served tea to the "weary travellers." It was very formal High Tea with tiny crustless cucumber sandwiches, then thick slabs of fresh gingerbread with butter melting on top, all served on fragile fine bone china. While the ladies pumped Percy William for news of the Bancroft branch of the clan, Margy studied her surroundings.

It would appear that once upon a time the Cousins'

house had been every bit as splendid as the larger house across the street. Everywhere were evidences of past splendour now slightly decayed: the faded velvet drapes festooned with silvery spider webs, the thick Persian carpets with the pattern worn off in the doorway, the heavy ornate silver forks with the dark tarnish between the tines. Perhaps the ancient Cousins didn't see the faded elegance around them. More likely they did see and preferred to ignore it, unable to keep up with the cost and care of maintaining their former grandeur. Margy liked them both so much already that it really didn't matter to her one way or the other.

As soon as Percy William departed for Belleville, Cousin Agnes and Cousin Annie were locked in mortal combat over who could spoil Margy the most. She was allowed to do what she liked, to sleep as late as she liked, and to eat as much as she could of the simple but elegant meals that the sisters prepared. Best of all there was no garden to water, weed and harvest, no beans to snap, and no preserving jars to scald.

Margy rapidly made friends with the four boys across the street, and quite covered herself with glory by "subbing" on Alex's baseball team, hitting a grand slam homer with the bases loaded.

Oh, but it was wonderful to just be "Margy, the girl visiting across the road," and nothing else. And it was wonderful to wander down the main street with Alex and not feel people watching her as she went by, and maybe even whispering delicately behind their hands after she passed.

Margy discovered that the boys' mother, Mrs. Brockman, was a widow who operated her large home as a "paying guest house," much the same way Mrs.-Strong-from-Fort-Stewart did. But this, thought Margy, was more like what she had in mind when she heard the description "fancy guest house." She was sure they didn't eat coarse oatmeal or tomatoes with brown sugar for breakfast.

The boys themselves said little about what it was like to live in the lovely home. Certainly they did their share of yard work, and carried bags in and out as the guests arrived or departed. But mainly their life consisted of baseball, baseball and baseball, with a little baseball thrown in on the side.

On the afternoon before Percy William was to drive her home, Margy played one last game of "pick-up" with the Brockman boys. At the end of the sixteenth inning Margy made her move to head back to "Blue Willows" across the street. She still had to repack her turkey.

Alex, the eldest of the brothers, dragged his attention away from the ratty ball he was tossing back and forth from hand to hand. "Oh, Margy," he said, rather as an unimportant aside, "Our Ma told us to ask you if you'd help her out tonight. One of the guests wants to have a fancy dinner party."

"Yeah," added the smallest brother, appropriately named Les, "She says she don't want us fellers bumbling around the dining room, slopping soup on the guests." He beamed as one well pleased that his incompetence had relieved him of this duty.

"Anyways," resumed Alex, "Ma says she'll pay you, and to be sure," (his voice assumed a charming falsetto), "to wear something pretty."

"She said to come over at four-thirty," added Les.

Their message thus satisfactorily relayed, the four boys sauntered off in the direction of the schoolyard where there was a real ball diamond and, with any luck, other fellows who would carry on from where they left off the day before.

Margy streaked across the road to "Blue Willows." It must be past four-thirty already. Those darn boys!

The Tummelty Cousins were prepared to allow Margy to help out their neighbour as a favour, but they cautioned Margy not to work too hard and overtire herself and not to accept any payment. Margy fled upstairs. She scrubbed her face and hands and put on the yellow organdy dress. Thank goodness she had taken it off right after church and it was still fresh and clean. She tied the ribbon sash carefully so the ends of the bow at the back were exactly the same length. Last of all she hurried out to the Cousins' overgrown garden and found a shaggy daisy which she managed to pin in her short hair. Then she hurried across the street.

Parked in front of the Guest House was the shiniest, most beautiful, glossy black "Model T" car Margy had ever seen. Mostly they just sat in crumbling decay in a farmer's field or behind a garage in the village. But this one had been restored to its glorious mint condition. And on the very top of its shining hood was a gigantic red bow, proclaiming to the world, or at least to Madoc, that this was a gift for a Very Special Person.

Margy knocked and then popped her head in at the back door of the Guest House. A pleasant-looking lady with the same sandy hair as the four boys looked up from the kitchen table where she was scraping potatoes.

"Oh, there you are at last, dear," she said. "I'm Mrs. Brockman. It's Margy, isn't it? The boys have told me all about you. My, don't you look nice. Let's tie an apron over your pretty dress and I'll put you to work."

Work indeed, but such very nice work that Margy loved it. Mrs. Brockman had the meal nearly all prepared so Margy was sent out to pick some flowers for the table and then arrange them in a large cut-glass bowl.

"But that's lovely, dear," said Mrs. Brockman enthusiastically when she saw Margy's efforts. "Boys know nothing about flowers. Send them out and they're likely to come back with goldenrod or dandelions . . . or not come back at all because they went off to play baseball." She laughed as if it didn't matter in the least.

They set the table together with all of Mrs. Brockman's finest linen and china, and fat red candles in brass candlesticks on both sides of Margy's flower bowl. The table looked gay and festive.

"Now then, Mr. . . . The Gentleman will sit here," Mrs. Brockman indicated the head of the table, "and His Lady will sit there." She pointed to a chair at the opposite end. "All the other paying guests will just sit wherever."

How very odd, thought Margy. This fancy dinner party and the guests are all just lodgers.

Mrs. Brockman caught her puzzled look. "Mr. . . . The Gentleman and His Lady are . . . *Americans,*" she said in a whisper, as if this explained everything.

"Oh," said Margy back in a hushed tone. Why the big secret, she thought. And why are we whispering? Were "The Gentleman and His Lady" gangsters . . . or fugitives of some sort?

"Did you see the fancy car outside?" Mrs. Brockman's mouth was very close to Margy's ear. "The Gentleman's birthday is in February but they're celebrating it now because . . . ." Her voice trailed off. "Well, just because," she said with finality. "Now, we'd better finish getting ready."

At the stroke of seven o'clock Mrs. Brockman asked Margy to ring the big gong in the kitchen that called the guests to dinner. As soon as they were seated in the dining room Mrs. Brockman came to the kitchen to collect Margy and begin the soup course. She smiled at Margy and said gaily, "Here we go. Remember, dear, serve from the right, clear from the left; ladies first and then gentlemen."

They removed their aprons and entered the dining room, Mrs. Brockman carrying the big tray. Margy followed her and carefully placed a steaming soup bowl in front of each guest.

There were only six guests. Margy was concentrating so hard on "serve-right-ladies-first" that she scarcely took in the pretty laughing lady with the cascade of blond hair at the end of the table, but as she set the soup bowl in front of her the Lovely Lady said, "Thank you, dear," in a voice like warm honey. Why did she look and sound so familiar? No time to think of that now. Serve-right-clear-left-ladies-first-then-gentlemen.

Not a drop of soup on the snowy linen. Not even a slosh of soup on the edge of a bowl. Margy set the last one down in front of the gentleman at the head of the table, and let out a sigh of relief.

"You did that just fine, sweetheart. I see you have a new helper tonight, Mrs. B."

Margy found herself staring right into the eyes of Mr. Clark Gable. The very same Clark Gable that she and Lenore had seen at the moving pictures that winter in *No Man of Her Own*. And the Lovely Lady at the other end of the table was Miss Lombard from the same movie. Margy stood rooted to the spot. She was glad that Mr. Gable hadn't asked her a question; she could not have framed a coherent answer to save her life.

Mrs. Brockman nodded smoothly and smiled. "And a good helper she is, Mr. Gable." She came briskly up behind Margy and propelled her bodily out the door.

In the safety of the kitchen Margy found her voice. "That's Clark Gable and Carole Lombard," she whispered through her hands which were clamped over her mouth.

"Yes, dear," said Mrs. Brockman serenely. "They're hiding here for a few days on a little 'escape holiday' by themselves."

That makes sense, thought Margy. What better place to hide from the world than Madoc? But what didn't make sense was that Margy was sure she had read in a magazine that Cora brought to an Order of the White Cloud meeting that Mr. Gable was married to someone else, and Miss Lombard had been too. At least that explained why Mrs. Brockman had been whispering. Not only were the two movie stars hiding away from the world on their "escape holiday," but also Mrs. Brockman wouldn't want her nice Guest House to get the reputation for accommodating couples who were not legally married to each other.

There wasn't time to do much more thinking about the situation right then, what with the serving and clearing, one course after another. The other four guests seemed almost as awestruck as Margy at being in the presence of such well-known personalities. But the guests of honour had a great time at their own party, right up to the giant birthday cake that Mrs. Brockman had made. It was rich chocolate with thick French vanilla icing and studded with thirty-two candles. Mr. Gable made Mrs. Brockman and Margy come in and have a piece of the cake too, and they all joined in singing "Happy Birthday, Mr. Gable."

After dinner all the paying guests squeezed into the birthday car and went for a "trial spin" around Madoc. Margy and Mrs. Brockman washed the dishes and discussed every detail of the dinner party. The boys arrived home from their baseball game at eight-thirty and finished off the cake before helping their mother and Margy tidy up. It was almost nine-thirty by the time everything was righted.

Margy refused Mrs. Brockman's offer to pay her, just as she had been instructed by the Cousins. She said politely, "Thank you, Mrs. Brockman, but helping you tonight was my pleasure," and she really meant it. Hadn't Mr. Gable called her "Sweetheart"? No matter what they thought of her in Bancroft, none of them, not even Gwennie, could say that Clark Gable had called her "Sweetheart." And that was something no one could ever take away from her. Just wait until she could tell the Order of the White Cloud!

Margy was packed and ready for Percy William when he arrived the next morning to take her home, although she couldn't find the yellow ribbon sash for her organdy dress. No mind, perhaps it had disappeared when she pulled her apron off last night in Mrs. Brockman's kitchen, and there wasn't time to go back and look.

It had been no use telling the Tummelty Cousins about her adventure; they had never been to a moving picture, not one that talked at any rate. But Percy William was highly impressed as she regaled him with the details all the way to Bannockburn.

The Aunts were delighted that Margy had such a good time in Madoc, even if they didn't know much about real movie stars either. (Margy discreetly referred to the Special Guests as "Mr. and Mrs. Gable" since she knew that the Aunts wouldn't know that they weren't— "Mr. and Mrs.," that is.)

"So you enjoyed yourself that much, Margy?" said Aunt Alice. "Didn't leave a 'Dutch anchor', did you?"

"What's that?" asked Margy.

"A 'Dutch anchor' is something you leave behind in a place you visit so you'll have an excuse to go back again someday," Aunt Alice explained. Margy thought about the yellow sash but said nothing. Aunt Alice knew everything anyway. A question popped into Margy's mind.

"Auntalice, 'Blue Willows' didn't look a thing like the big house at the bottom of the Blue Willow platter," she said as respectfully as possible.

"Of course not," said Aunt Alice shortly. "That's the 'Chinese Temple'. 'Blue Willows' looks like the little house halfway up the plate."

Margy immediately got out the platter and looked at it again. Yes, of course, Aunt Alice was right.

Aunt Alice was always right.

CHAPTER

——10——

In late August, as soon as the weather turned cool, Aunt Edith began her yearly ritual of practising her bread-making to perfect her entry in the Bancroft Fall Fair. Margy found this frenzy of "practising" curious indeed, since Aunt Edith made bread every week, year in and year out, the best bread in the whole wide world. But every year Aunt Edith renewed her determination to win the local competition. She said that she would "rather win in Bancroft than at the Royal Winter Fair or the Canadian Exhibition."

Margy felt a little wounded that her very first day of Continuation School came and went largely uncelebrated. There were any number of things to discuss: the two new teachers that shared the responsibility of teaching the First Form; the exotic new subjects like Algebra and Latin and French and Social Studies; the fact that so many of Margy's classmates from the previous year were gone, replaced by new students from the outlying communities whose families were able to afford the extra cost of books and lodging so their sons or daughters could go on to higher education. Of course Aunt Alice was highly interested in these exciting details but even she deferred to her sister's single-minded devotion to making the perfect loaf of bread for the fair. No matter where the dinner table conversation started out, it *always* ended up with bread-baking.

There were, however, certain compensations. The Fine House was constantly filled with the wonderful smell of baking bread, and there were always lots of fresh samples to "test."

Margy couldn't tell the difference from one batch to the next, but Aunt Edith and Aunt Alice had long discussions on the optimum length of rising time to give the most uniform texture on the inside of each loaf, or on what temperature the oven should be to give the best crust on the outside. In the meantime Margy just sat back and enjoyed the delicious bread, warm and indigestible from the oven with butter melting down through it. And Aunt Edith was far too distracted to notice how many lashings of jam Margy smeared on the top.

The prize for the "best loaf of bread" entered in the Fall Fair was donated by the Sunshine Yeast Company. It consisted of a year's supply of Sunshine yeast for the talented winner. A package of the yeast was to be displayed beside each entry, along with a receipt from the grocery store to prove that the contestant had in fact bought and used the right kind of yeast in the baking of her bread. The scrupulously honest Aunt Edith had dutifully purchased ten packets of Sunshine yeast, even though it was not her regular brand. She pronounced it "weak and unreliable" and Margy knew that the minute the fair was over her Aunt would revert to the familiar blue and red package of

Golden Grain yeast which was her constant baking day companion. Margy wondered what Aunt Edith would *do* with a year's supply of the "weak and unreliable" brand when she won the contest, for Margy had no doubt that she would win. After all, wasn't she practising with Sunshine yeast until her bread was perfect?

After lunch, and before she went back to school, Margy cut another slice of fresh bread and opened up the *Bancroft Times* on the kitchen table. She spread it to the page that had all the news about the Fall Fair which was to be held that weekend. If only there were some competition she could enter and win, especially if the prize was money. Then she could begin to fill her almost empty money box again; Christmas was less than four months away.

Not only that, but she would dearly love to be the best at something, at *anything*. Then the other kids would just have to sit up and admire her. Coming second in the Entrances was good, but not good enough. And if Gwennie had been upset about Margy's winning Mr. Warren's red pencil in the grammar contest last June . . . well, Gwennie could just *eat her dust* when the Fall Fair prizes were announced. But first she would have to find something she could be best at.

Margy smoothed the newspaper and began at the top of the page, working her way methodically down through the lists. Of course, all the major categories were out of the question: things like horses, cattle, poultry, root vegetables, and grain. Anyway, the prizes for these categories were not very exciting, usually things like "a half-gallon of dip and disinfectant," or "a five-gallon pail of honey."

The Domestic Science categories held a bit more promise, but again, a person had to actually be *good* at something in order to enter and win.

The local tinsmith had donated a prize of six assorted handmade cookie cutters for the "best loaf of raisin bread." Margy pointed this category out to Aunt Edith just in case she wanted to enter that contest as well.

"Humph," said Aunt Edith. "That's 'Little Abe' Conners. He just likes raisin bread. He'll donate the prize—which he can make out of scraps in less than an hour—and then after the judging is over collect the entries and live on raisin bread for the next week. Why, he'll think he's died and gone to heaven."

Margy had seen Little Abe, the massive town smithy, outside his tiny bachelor cottage beside the forge. She thought it extremely clever of him to get ten or twelve loaves of his favourite bread in this ingenious manner.

Her eye moved down the list. There were prizes for all manner of baking, as well as for domestic needlecraft, sewing, knitting, crocheting, rug hooking and braiding, and quilting. In the "Artistic Endeavours" category a prize of two dollars was offered for the "best collection of five original oil paintings." Margy was quite sure she could come up with five great oil paintings by Friday—this was only Tuesday—using Aunt Alice's oils, but this was likely to be a popular and crowded category since half the young ladies in the village took lessons in art and decorum from the church organist. It was all very discouraging.

Then she saw it.

The very last category, tucked in at the bottom of the page underneath an advertisement for Crown's liniment: Categories twenty and twenty-one, "For Boys and Girls."

"Donated by the Hunter Manufacturing Company, Makers of English Military Oil and Cough Syrup, first prize, five dollars; second prize, three dollars; third prize, one dollar, for the best birdhouse made by a boy up to the age of fifteen," and "Donated by C. D. Tanner Ice Cream and Confectionery, one five-pound box of chocolates, for the best handmade apron, made by a girl up to the age of fifteen."

Margy couldn't believe her luck. Not only a category just for her, but something she felt sure she could do.

She would build a birdhouse!

So what if this was a category for boys? Boys always got to do the good stuff—like play hookey from school and go fishing, or play baseball and hockey, or build birdhouses. Well, Margy would just build a real humdinger and get it into the competition somehow.

None of the other Fall Fair categories were designated for men or women only. Both could enter the animal husbandry competitions, or the flowers, or even the baking. Hadn't Aunt Edith been furious last year when a man had won the bread-baking category? And Margy decided that she herself would be more than pleased if a boy chose to enter an apron and then won the box of chocolates. So there.

Yes, it was settled. Margy would build a birdhouse and enter it secretly in the boys' competition. After all, the prize was for the best birdhouse. Why should anyone care *who* built it? The birds certainly wouldn't. And a fair should be fair!

That very afternoon after school, while Aunt Alice was at the library and Aunt Edith was having a snooze upstairs following a strenuous day of baking, Margy slipped down to the cellar. There were lots of bits of wood in the corner, and Grandfather's few tools still hung on neat hooks along one wall above the sturdy work bench.

Margy had no idea how to build a birdhouse so she just started right in. In the end it was not difficult. She experimented with bits of wood, propping them together different ways until something that approximated the picture she had in her mind took shape. The saw was long and cumbersome but Margy struggled with it until it behaved properly. A basic box shape with a charming sloped roof evolved. Margy drilled a neat doorway hole with Grandfather's brace and bit and then attached a fake chimney to the roof for effect.

In a dusty corner she found some ancient pots of paint that still sloshed when she shook them. She painted her birdhouse a bright red with a white roof and shutters. Then she hid it in the cold room and banged the lids back on the paint tins. She could hear Aunt Edith moving around above, getting supper started.

Margy slipped like a shadow upstairs to the bathroom to clean up. This building of birdhouses was a messy business, all sawdust and paint speckles. But it was worth it. She was ever so pleased at the results of her efforts. It was a very good birdhouse, and she had made it all herself.

When she finally appeared to set the table for supper, Aunt Edith said, "What on earth were you doing down there?"

"Oh, just tidying up, Auntedith," replied Margy airily. It was a sign of how tired and distracted Aunt Edith was that she didn't question this remarkable statement further. And fortunately Aunt Alice had been polishing furniture earlier that day with her favourite linseed oil and turpentine mixture so they didn't even notice the smell of paint.

The next day Margy searched for someone to enter the birdhouse at the fair for her. But George was absent and Snuffy was entering one of his own. By the time school was out for the day she was desperate. She might have to enter the birdhouse on her own and risk being disqualified simply for being a girl. Otherwise she would just have to abandon the whole idea altogether and miss her chance for the prize money. And the glory.

As Margy pulled on her jacket at the back of the room, alone as usual, she gave a profound sigh of disappointment and frustration.

Suddenly a deep voice beside her said, "Whatsa matter, kid?" Ralph had come back for his baseball mitt. Margy looked at him in voiceless confusion. He persisted, "Is something wrong, Margy?"

Margy found her tongue and plunged. "I built a birdhouse for the fair, but I have to find a boy to enter it for me," she said rather defiantly, challenging him to tell her she couldn't, or shouldn't, or simply laugh at her.

But Ralph did none of these. "A birdhouse," he said thoughtfully. "That's real swell, Margy." Then,

"Couldn't find a boy to enter it? So what am I, a ham sandwich?"

"Oh, Ralph, would you?"

Ralph said easily, "Sure. I'll just enter it in my name and see what happens. You get it to me Friday after school and I'll take it up to the fairgrounds." He grinned in a conspiratorial way and turned to go. Then he turned back towards her as if reluctant to leave. "Is it a good birdhouse?" he asked.

"Great," said Margy with conviction. She didn't want Ralph to think he had to enter something second-rate under his name.

"What colour?"

"Mostly red," said Margy, her face the same colour.

"My favourite colour," said Ralph.

"Yes," said Margy. "Mine too." She wanted to add, "Just like the braces I gave you." But then that would give her away as his Secret Friend.

"Well . . . ," said Ralph.

"Well . . . ," said Margy.

He turned towards the door a second time. "I'd best be going. The fellers will be wondering what happened to me."

"Yes," said Margy. Then quickly, "Thanks for helping me out. I was afraid I wouldn't be able to . . . you know . . . enter the contest."

"That's okay, kid. I hope you win," said Ralph. He disappeared out the door and was gone. Margy sighed again. But this time it was not a sigh of disappointment.

Thursday night she gave the birdhouse its finishing touches while the Aunts were out at a card party. From various pots of paint she added tiny window frames and curtains, and a bold row of flowers across the front and around the door. The following morning she put it into a cardboard carton and hid it in the shed.

Immediately after school she gave it to Ralph and he set off to enter it. Just as he went around the corner of the Fine House Aunt Alice came up the hill, back from dropping off Aunt Edith's loaf of bread at the fair. Margy held her breath as they passed but thankfully Aunt Alice didn't stop to talk to Ralph, who simply shifted the carton to his other arm and lifted his cap politely.

That evening was the longest Friday night in recorded history. Margy wandered by herself up to the fairgrounds to look around but the building where all the displays were was closed to the public while the judges were inside deciding on the winners. Word was all over town that the judges had arrived on the six o'clock train from Out Front.

There were two gentleman judges and one lady judge, all appointed by the Ontario Government to do the circuit of the county fairs and make impartial, objective decisions which would render to the competitions a justice not attainable by local judges who knew all the contestants personally. The two men would judge the livestock and crop exhibits, while the lady judge would do the domestic crafts, floral displays, baking, and art.

Rumour also had it that the gentlemen judges would assess the birdhouses and the lady judge the apron competition. Margy wished she hadn't painted the flowers on the outside of her house. That would never appeal to a man judge. Too late now to do anything about it. She also heard that there were no fewer than fourteen entries in the birdhouse competition, from boys all over the north end of the county. It was hard not to be discouraged.

As Margy left the fairgrounds dusk had enveloped the village. She met Snuffy, Jane and Cora who were also heading back to town. They had come up to the fairgrounds to see if the cotton candy stand was open. When they met up with Margy they had just decided to look in on the dance at the Community Hall. The toe-tapping music could be heard halfway to the fairgrounds, and everyone they met as they walked through town was moving in that direction, like moths toward a bright light.

"Now we can only stay a minute," cautioned Cora. "Our mother told us we had to be home by nine or she wouldn't let us go to the fair tomorrow until after noon. And," she added importantly, "I'm going to help the man who's running the candy apple stand. He asked me tonight if I'd like a job." She turned to Margy. "You want to help too, Margy? He said he had a job for two or three until his nieces who usually help him arrive on the Excursion Train from Out Front. And Jane doesn't want to do it."

Want to help! But of course Margy did. Imagine working in a booth at the fair and having people say, "I'll have two candied apples, Miss." If they wanted an apple they would darn well *have* to talk to her, and nicely, too. Margy nodded happily.

The dance at the Community Hall was a crush of couples of all ages. To many people in the village and beyond, this event was the highlight of the Fall Fair.

The music and laughter, the colourful dresses, and the bright electric lights in the hall all combined to produce a tingle in the air. Cora, Jane, Snuffy and Margy threaded their way through the crowd at the entrance to the hall.

The sign at the door said, "Ladies—free: Gents—five cents a dance." How in Heaven's name, wondered Margy, would they ever figure out who had paid for what dance and who had not.

The music, a skittish ragtime number provided by a local band, rose to a rippling climax and dwindled in the applause that followed. Two men standing just in front of the stage stretched a thick rope across the width of one end of the hall and then walked slowly towards the other end, drawing the good-natured dancers with them. As soon as the floor was cleared in this manner, the "gents" began to shove their nickels at the two attendants to let them back under the rope with their ladies.

At that moment the band decided to take a break. As the members headed off to have a smoke or a drink of lemonade, a tall curly-headed boy took over the piano. A smattering of applause greeted his entrance. Margy recognized him from one of the higher forms at the Continuation School. He was extremely talented on the piano, but from a very poor family out on the Winter Road. Because he had no sheet music to practise, just his mother's old hymn book, he played only church music—but in dance tempo. He started out with "Faith of Our Fathers" played in waltz time. Several older couples paid their nickels to join the growing crowd on the dance floor. Someone turned the electric lights down a bit.

Margy watched the swaying crowd move in stately parade past her. Someday that would be her out there, moving in perfect time to the music with some handsome fellow. One-two-three, one-two-three. She had never actually been asked to dance before, but she and Cora had practised at an Order of the White Cloud meeting, right after they had seen Fred Astaire and Joan Crawford in *Dancing Lady* at the movies earlier that year. Yes, someday, thought Margy, closing her eyes . . . *one-two-three, one-two-three* . . .

"Wanna dance, kid?" said Ralph's voice, right in front of her. Her eyes flew open. Not the most elegant invitation in history, but Margy's first. Cora gave her a nudge and Margy followed Ralph onto the floor. Thank goodness it was a slow dance and she had no trouble following his lead.

Ralph leaned his cheek against her hair and whispered something in her ear. Margy strained to hear. She did not want to miss a single moment of this romantic encounter.

"I said, I got it in okay," repeated Ralph. "Your birdhouse. I got it in to the competition."

"Oh," said Margy.

"Yeah," said Ralph. "The ladies marking the entries thought it was real swell."

Oh, sure, thought Margy, the ladies did, but how would the men judges feel.

"I thought you'd like to know," said Ralph. He subsided into silence and Margy savoured the rest of the dance. Who cared if he just asked her so he could pass on the message? Right here in front of everyone she was dancing with Ralph.

And doing a pretty good job too. The music shifted from the waltz to a saucy foxtrot ("Just a Closer Walk with Thee") without stopping, and they shifted and swayed along with the best of them. Finally the melody trailed off and the dancers gave the young pianist a rousing round of applause. The men with the rope began their ritual of clearing the floor. Margy wondered if Ralph would ask her for another dance but he merely said, "Thanks, kid. See you tomorrow at the fair," and sauntered off in the direction of his friends, chief among whom seemed to be Gwennie who was holding up a glass of lemonade she had bought for him.

Margy tried to hide her disappointment at not being asked for another dance and waved gaily after him before she was swept away by the men with their rope. She decided she would not wait around to see if he danced with anyone else but would start for home.

Margy caught up to Cora and Jane who were also heading out the door. Cora gave Margy an admiring look and squeezed her hand. She mouthed the word "Ralph" and fluttered her eyelashes at Margy. Margy blushed and tried to look nonchalant.

Saturday dawned one of those perfect Bancroft Fall Fair days: bright sunshine and a blue sky punctuated with cottony clouds, the kind of clouds that make you want to lie dreamily on your back and make up stories about them. But who had time for that today?

Margy met Cora at eight by the booth on the fairgrounds. A tall skinny man and his short plump wife got them organized for the candy apple production.

Margy was to sort, wash and dry the apples and put the sticks in them. The plump wife then plunged them into the boiling red toffee and put them on buttered sheets to set. Once they were cool, Cora wrapped them carefully in waxed paper with the sticks poking up, and sold them to the customers at the front of the booth. Having got the women all organized, the tall skinny husband disappeared to enjoy the fair. By nine o'clock they had a good supply ahead and people were already buying them, walking away from the booth sucking happily on their sticky treat.

All morning Margy thought about her birdhouse and played games with herself to decide if she had really won. If the next man to buy a candy apple is wearing braces, I won. (He wasn't.) If the next lady to buy an apple is wearing a hat, I won. (She was wearing a scarf tied over her hair. Was that a hat or not?) If the next person to buy a candy apple is a little girl, I won. (It was! Well, not really a young girl, but definitely small in stature.)

Finally, about noon, the Excursion Train from Out Front arrived and the fairground was flooded with a sea of people, among whom were the candy apple man's nieces who took over from Cora and Margy. They gladly surrendered their aprons and melted into the crowd, sucking their complimentary apples and clutching their quarter dollars that the plump wife had paid them for their morning's work.

"Let's go and look at the exhibits," said Margy eagerly.

But no, Cora wanted to go over to where the drawing contests were already under way in front of the grandstand. Splendid huge horses, curried and groomed to gleaming perfection, were pitted against one another in drawing a raft-looking affair piled high with stones. Their owners, each determined that his team was the most powerful, urged the beautiful animals to their limit. As soon as the drawing contest was over and the blue silk ribbon pinned on the harness of a magnificent Percheron, the "Quick Hitch-up Contest" began. Quite a large crowd gathered on the bleachers since this was the amusing climax of the morning events.

The judge bellowed out the rules of the contest. "The contestants will start with the stable halter on their animal. They will then unhalter, and proceed to bridle and harness it with collar and hames but not snaps, hitch it to their buggy, walk once around the track, trot once around the track, and then unharness the animal and replace the stable halter. The prize for this contest," (he consulted his list), "The prize for this contest is one horse blanket, donated by Rainer's Hardware Store."

They were off to catcalls and good-natured encouragement from the audience. The horses, made skittish by the noise and confusion and haste, were most uncooperative, but in the end the bay horse that Cora had picked won. Only then did she allow herself to be dragged away to the exhibit barns.

The displays were set up in long low buildings which had served as barracks when the fairgrounds had been a training base during the Great War. Because the buildings were rather narrow it was difficult to work one's way through the crush of people admiring the displays. Cora and Margy edged their way through the crowd that jammed the aisle area. Generally speaking, people were forgiving as the two girls threaded their way among the throng, trying not to step on any toes along the way. They drew back with a smile at Cora's "'Scuse me, 'scuse me." Was it Margy's imagination, or was that smile for Cora replaced by a cool aloofness when the person saw who was following her? Always, thought Margy, there's that glass wall of reserve between me and everyone else. Always. Always.

The girls edged past the flower displays to the baking. Margy saw the Sunshine Yeast bread-baking area and noted that Aunt Edith's bread had the red ribbon for second prize pinned to it. But the blue first prize ribbon was on Mr. Greer's loaf again. Aunt Edith would not be happy about that.

Finally the two girls approached the end of the building where the children's entries were displayed. A group of Form Oners were clustered around a table. Margy could see Ralph's tall frame at the hub of the group, and she heard Gwennie's shrill and excited voice.

"Oh, Ralph, what are you going to do with all that money?"

Margy pushed her way to the front. Yes, there was her beautiful red birdhouse with a beautiful blue ribbon pinned on it. She had to bite her lip from shouting out loud. Ralph caught her eye and grinned. At that moment a tall, angular woman emerged from the crowd of adults and wrapped her arms around Ralph.

"Oh, Ralphie, I'm *so* proud of you!"

"Gee willikers, Ma," said Ralph, trying to disentangle

himself, but he grinned affectionately at her.

Margy and Cora left the group (which now included Lenore and Snuffy, as well as Jane and Gwennie, still clinging to Ralph's arm and trying to decide how he should spend the prize money). The two girls moved off to enjoy the rest of the fair, George tagging along with them.

The three inspected all the displays, exhibits and animals again. They patronized the games area where men in loud checkered suits tried to entice them to "spend money to make money." They took in the baseball game in front of the bleachers and cheered loudly for the home team. (It was an exciting game: Bancroft 13, Boulter 34.) They ate popcorn and cotton candy and washed it down with root beer. Margy spent almost a dollar, but after all she had won five.

They all parted at dusk, feeling they had truly "done the fair." The cool September evening was closing in and the full moon was rising. Ralph caught up to Margy just as she was leaving and whispered, "I'll go and collect the prize money and bring it to you."

A half-hour later he was indeed ringing the brass doorbell of the Fine House. Margy stepped out onto the porch in the moonlight. Ralph put the beautiful crisp five-dollar bill into her hand. It was the first one Margy had ever held.

"It was a great birdhouse, Margy," he whispered, standing very close to her.

Bang! The porch light glared on and Aunt Alice appeared in the doorway.

"Oh, it's you, Ralph. Why don't you ask him in, Margy?" Then, "Ralph, we saw your birdhouse.

Congratulations. I didn't know you were so artistic. You certainly deserve . . . ." Aunt Alice's voice dwindled as she studied the five-dollar bill in Margy's hand. "What is going on here?"

"Well, you see . . . ." Ralph waded in bravely. "Well, that is . . . like . . . you see."

"And I . . . well, I . . . you see . . . ." elaborated Margy.

"Yes," said Aunt Alice, "I think I do see. You made the birdhouse, didn't you, Margy?"

Margy and Ralph nodded in mournful unison.

"And you entered it in Ralph's name."

Again a slow nod.

"Well," briskly, "it will say in the *Bancroft Times* that Ralph won. Ralph's mother thinks he won. I expect the *honest* thing to do would be to give the prize money back to Ralph. I'm sure that will be penance enough for both of you."

"But, Miss Mullett . . . ," said Ralph.

"But, Auntalice . . . ," pleaded Margy.

"But me no buts, either one of you," said Aunt Alice firmly.

There was no arguing with Aunt Alice when she had that tone in her voice. Margy reluctantly handed the money to Ralph. Ralph reluctantly took it.

Aunt Alice held the door open for Margy. Ralph smiled ruefully at them both, lifted his cap and backed away. Margy preceded Aunt Alice into the house and started up the stairs with dragging feet and empty pockets.

Aunt Alice called her back. "I'm sorry you're disappointed, Margy," she said slowly. "That was an awful lot of money for you."

"I *did* win it," said Margy, "fair and square."

"Hardly 'fair and square,'" said Aunt Alice gently, "if you entered a competition not intended for you and used someone else's name."

Margy had to admit this was true.

"By now the whole town thinks Ralph won the contest. If people start hearing that you cooked up this affair it won't do your reputation for honesty any good, will it?"

Again Margy had to admit this was true. She was already trying to live down one false accusation. She didn't need to have people think she was sneaky all over again. Margy sighed. "It's still not fair," she said.

"No," agreed Aunt Alice, "it isn't fair. You should have been able to enter that birdhouse in your own name and win, all up front and proper. But sometimes life isn't fair. It makes rules that aren't fair but if you break them . . . you just find yourself in more trouble."

Aunt Alice looked as tired and disappointed as Margy felt. Margy knew that life certainly hadn't treated Aunt Alice very fairly, but she never gave up trying to do the right and honest thing. But sometimes, it seemed that even to Aunt Alice "honest" and "right" were not always the same thing. Aunt Alice hadn't insisted that Margy confess to the judges what she had done; she had simply asked her to give the money back to Ralph. Aunt Alice had not been, strictly speaking, "honest," but she had tried to do what she thought was right in the face of several layers of injustice.

Margy was suddenly struck by a thought. She remembered how strange she had felt when she was trying to tell Mr. Warren about Orlie. Maybe telling on Orlie would have been the *honest* thing, but maybe it wasn't the right thing to do after all. And maybe all this meant that she was beginning to think and act the way Aunt Alice did. The thought pleased her.

Suddenly it was important to Margy to let Aunt Alice know that it was all right to lose the five dollars if, in Aunt Alice's opinion, it was the right thing to do.

Margy pasted a smile on her face and looked Aunt Alice in the eye. "Anyway," she said proudly to her Aunt, "it was a good birdhouse."

Aunt Alice pulled herself up to her full diminutive height. "It was," she said, "a *great* birdhouse."

CHAPTER
—11—

Chautauqua!

  The word itself was enough to send a grateful
shiver up the spine of every man, woman and child in
Bancroft. This would be Margy's very first Chautauqua,
but Lenore had told her all about it so her spine could
tingle too, along with everyone else's.

  According to Lenore, the troupe of travelling
Chautauqua entertainers would descend upon the
community for a four-day extravaganza of various shows.
And this was not merely amateur talent either. These
were truly professional performers who went from
community to community giving entertainments that the
local people would never see unless they went to a
fancy theatre in Toronto or Ottawa or Montreal.

  Not that Bancroft didn't have its share of talented
performers. There were several first-rate bands in the
area, and hardly a month went by without some church
or community group getting up a play or concert of
some kind to entertain the public and raise some
money for a Good Cause. These efforts always received
splendid reviews in the *Bancroft Times*.

  And rightly so. The comic plays were always funnier

if one knew all the actors. Why, the whole village was still talking about the Minstrel Show Benefit that had been mounted by some men of the community two or three years earlier. By all reports the entire cast was stricken with a severe case of stage fright minutes before the show, the only remedy for which was that the director administer quantities of "liquid courage" in the form of homemade liquor. The result was the shortest but most totally unforgettable medley of Stephen Foster favourites in the history of live theatre. During the opening number, one man in the first row laughed so hard he had an apoplectic fit, three ladies in the audience fainted, and eight others had to be helped from the auditorium.

Apparently they were unaware of the alternative lyrics to "I Dream of Jeannie with the Light Brown Hair," made popular in the trenches of the Great War. Certainly the ladies had never heard that particular rendition of "De Campdown Races" which mentioned by name two "widows" out the Mud Road. Still, since no one asked for their money back, the event had raised eleven dollars and twenty cents for the Red Cross Society.

Yes, the local entertainers were many and colourful. But this was the Chautauqua! And extra special this year since they had not come last fall at all. Even before the posters went up the whole Continuation School was abuzz with anticipation. Some of the girls were getting new dresses for the occasion. Margy wasn't, since the yellow organdy (with a new ribbon sash) still fit quite well.

Finally the posters went up. Margy and Lenore

walked downtown right after school to read them.

"Four big days!" screamed the large poster at the Post Office. "Seven unique programmes! Only $1.75 for adults, $1 for children, for the whole series." Aunt Alice had already said that Margy should have her own ticket and go to every event, while she and Aunt Edith would share a ticket and each go to half.

Margy was most excited about the plays. One was described as "a powerful and poignant drama of simple folk plunged into a vortex of emotional conflict by the advent of the Great War." Margy had never seen anyone plunged into a vortex of anything and she could hardly wait. The second play was a romantic comedy involving "a greedy man and his invalid daughter, and a tinker who mended not only pots and pans, but hearts and lives as well." Aunt Edith said it sounded like a "three-handkerchief" play to her.

As well as the plays there would be a singing group called "Sorrentino and His Venetian Strollers," a marionette show, a magician, a lecturer speaking on "Life at the Bottom of the Sea," and finally, as the climax, a world-famous concert pianist, Herr Gunter Matthias Braun, who would give the closing performance. The posters blared in crooked capitals: "Herr Braun will give you AN EVENING YOU WILL NEVER FORGET! Direct from BERLIN, PARIS, and NEW YORK to BANCROFT!" It was nice to see little Bancroft mentioned in print in the very same sentence as Paris and New York, rather like their cosy village was internationally important after all.

Margy confessed to Lenore that she wasn't very excited about anything on the programme except the plays. The rest sounded pretty tedious, especially the lecturer and the pianist.

"Oh, no, Margy," Lenore reassured her, *"Everything* at the Chautauqua is wonderful. Why, two years ago there was a retired judge who talked about 'Criminal Law in Early Ontario'. I thought that would be pretty boring but it was great, all about hatchet murders and lynchings."

Margy had to admit that did sound attractive, and she was pleasantly surprised when this year's lecturer held the crowd spellbound for almost two hours with his descriptions of strange and wonderful underwater creatures. He even touched on the lost city of Atlantis and pointed out its location on a large wall map. Margy and Aunt Alice listened carefully so they could tell Aunt Edith all about it when they got home.

The whole school walked over to the Community Hall to watch the caped magician "Marvello" who entertained and amazed his audience with his conjuring and card tricks. He even asked for a volunteer from the audience to be sawn in half, but no one offered so in the end he had to use his beautiful assistant, Miss Gina the Gypsy princess. Margy never took her eyes off the stage but suddenly there were the two halves of Miss Gina in two separate boxes and the next minute she was back together again, smiling and bowing. The room was filled with the shrill cheers of two hundred school children as well as hearty applause from the many adults who crammed in at the back, enjoying the show at least as much as the younger audience.

The marionette show was also splendid. They did "Jack and the Beanstalk" and "Goldilocks and the

Three Bears." The bear puppets were wonderful: even their mouths opened and closed jerkily when they talked. When Papa Bear said, "Who's been sleeping in *my* bed?" in his gruff and growly voice, a little girl in the front row covered her face with her pinafore and screamed, "Not me!" and everyone in the audience laughed.

Oh, but it was a glorious week! Before Margy knew it the Chautauqua visit was almost over. She and Aunt Edith got to the Community Hall early on Saturday evening for the final sell-out performance of the famous concert pianist. They found two seats on the aisle near the front and took possession of them. After they were seated and settled comfortably, Margy looked around.

Oh, no! They were sitting directly behind the large and rowdy Marker family. Orlie himself was right in front of her, arm-wrestling with the brother, probably Archibald, who was sitting next to him. Beside him and moving down the row were Raymond, Cline, Lorelei, Veronica, Launcelot, and finally Little Sammy sitting beside his mother. Mrs. Marker sat with one arm encircling Little Sammy protectively, and in the crook of her other arm held a new and noisy baby.

Orlie looked up from his contest of strength and caught sight of Margy. Immediately the hooded expression dropped over his eyes. He shook his head as if to clear it and assumed a brazen front. "Hi ya, Margy," he said, a little too loudly. "How are ya doing?"

Margy glared back. He knew darned well how she was doing. She nudged Aunt Edith who was already deep in conversation with the person on the other side of her. "Can we move somewhere else?" Margy whispered, loudly enough for Orlie to hear. "I don't like the view from here," she added pointedly.

Aunt Edith looked incredulous. "But these are excellent seats, Margy," she said a little impatiently. "We were lucky to get the last two places together so near the front. Why can't you see? There's only that nice young man in front of you." She turned back to her conversation.

At the words "nice young man" Orlie grinned saucily at Margy, apparently confident now that he knew she had never told even her Aunt about her suspicion of him. He stuck out his tongue, and returned to his arm wrestling.

Margy looked determinedly away from Orlie. She was not going to let him spoil the last Chautauqua concert.

Her eyes drifted around the Community Hall. It was a lovely hall, as nice as any hall the Chautauqua players could have visited, with its glossy hardwood floors and polished panelling, the wide balcony at the back and spacious stage at the front, shrouded by the heavy dark curtain made of canvas on narrow wooden slats which rolled down from the ceiling. That curtain was the pride of the community. It featured a hand-painted scene from Mr. Wallace's famous book, *Ben-Hur:* a triple-life-size depiction of the race scene, complete with rearing horses, careening chariots, bulging muscles and cracking whips. One could sit and admire its detail before the show began and during the intermissions.

Yes, it was a community hall of which to be proud,

and the expectant murmur of the well-behaved audience reflected this pride.

It was somehow important to Margy that their Community Hall be fine enough for the visiting entertainers. The troupe had no doubt played in the finest concert halls in the world. How terrible if they felt that Bancroft were not up to their standard, or worse yet, laughed behind their hands at little Bancroft after they left. It was especially important tonight, the closing night of Chautauqua, always the most spectacular with the brightest star.

No one had actually seen Herr Braun yet, but the village was rife with rumour. At the Post Office Margy had heard that the great pianist was an eccentric recluse who had not left his hotel room since arriving in Bancroft. At Rainer's Hardware Store she heard that he had gone over to try the old grand piano in the Community Hall, peremptorily declared it appalling and demanded that it be tuned *immediately*. And once it was tuned no one was to be allowed to so much as touch it until after his concert was over. Perhaps, thought Margy, he makes the same demands in Paris and New York. Her eyes travelled around the hall again for reassurance.

Mr. Cooper of Cooper's Emporium, one of the local businessmen who had sponsored the Chautauqua visit, appeared on the stage in front of the closed curtain. (Margy scrunched down in her seat.) Mr. Cooper welcomed the crowd and went on at length about how proud and privileged they should all feel to have an artist of Herr Braun's capabilities in their humble midst. The audience applauded his remarks enthusiastically.

(Margy did not applaud. She would never forgive Mr. Cooper for telling Verna that she couldn't be her friend any more.)

Finally Mr. Cooper remembered what he was out there to do and got around to introducing Herr Braun. The pianist stepped out from the side door and climbed the few steps to the stage.

He was a short, stocky man with a great deal of bushy black hair sticking out in all directions. His bristly black eyebrows nearly met across the bridge of his wide German nose. The coat tails of his severe black suit dangled below his bandy knees, and his black leather shoes shone like mirrors.

He acknowledged the uncertain applause with a jerk of a bow. His eyes swept the room with a cold stare, then he turned abruptly. The heavy curtain rose revealing the grand piano alone in the centre of the stage, a sheaf of music propped up on it. Herr Braun crossed the stage smartly and sat down at the piano, flipping his coat tails out behind him. He shifted the bench slightly to the left, opened the music on the rack, and without further introduction launched into the first piece.

Play? My, yes, he could play. Crashing chords and frantic arpeggios that clawed their way right from the bottom to the top of the keyboard and right off the end it seemed. Sometimes it sounded as if three hands were on the keyboard, if not four. The pianist could flip the pages of music before him with either hand and in the middle of a crashing sequence without missing a note or breaking his unblinking concentration. And the music! Wild and resonant, or heavy and brooding. Very powerful . . . very angry . . . very German.

After each piece was finished the audience responded with timid applause. Herr Braun paid no attention whatsoever and launched into his next piece of music, sometimes without even waiting for their weak response to die away.

Everyone in the audience seemed a little relieved when the curtain rang down for the intermission. The audience sat in cowed silence for a moment. Then the mutter of conversation sprang up throughout the hall. Some of the gentlemen disappeared out the main door to have a smoke on the steps of the hall. The women twisted in their seats to chat with others around them about the weather, the price of bread, their children. Margy didn't hear anyone discussing the concert. What was there to say?

Aunt Edith had moved over and was chatting with Mrs. Marker about the high cost of rearing children in these hard times, as if they were great friends from way back. How could Aunt Edith just sit there and talk in such a friendly manner with someone she had specifically described as "Not Our Kind?" A blush warmed Margy's face at the memory of her Aunt's superior comment. Apparently at least for this evening the laws of neighbourliness overrode any misgivings Aunt Edith might have about the suitability of conversation with a Marker. If she only knew what Orlie Marker had done. Then she would really feel that family was "Not Our Kind." Margy's flush of embarrassment was replaced by the familiar ache of anger and frustration.

She got out of her seat and wandered down the centre aisle. Everyone else her age and under was strolling about too. Small knots of friends appeared around the edges of the hall. All the young Markers, from Orlie right down to Little Sammy, had scattered in various directions. Margy saw Lenore talking to Verna on the other side of the room, so she changed her direction for a group of boys near the door. Ralph was among them and she thought she could glimpse the scarlet Christmas braces under his best Sunday-go-to-meeting jacket. She wanted to stroll past close enough to find out for sure.

Margy skirted the edge of the crowd, pretending she wanted to step out the door for a breath of fresh air. At the precisely correct moment she changed tack and hooked around towards the water fountain. Just as she was about to turn back towards her seat and take a *good look* at Ralph on the way, Orlie appeared at her elbow.

Apparently he had decided to mend bridges, now that he felt the safety and separation of over nine months since the Christmas Cheer incident. Probably, thought Margy, when Aunt Edith didn't change seats when I asked her to, he figured that "everybody has most forgotten."

Orlie leaned companionably against the wall by the water fountain and chatted to Margy in a rambling, non-stop way as if there had never been any problem between them. He told her all about the calf he was raising on his own on his Pa's farm, and how he might get a real job next spring on his aunt's farm near Sudbury. Margy shifted from foot to foot and tried to plot her escape. When she looked again the group of boys at the door had disappeared. Apparently they were not staying for the second half of the concert. By now they were no doubt circling in on Mr. McAdam's apple trees.

It was a long intermission. When the electric lights finally flickered to call people back Margy was grateful. At least she could get away from Orlie. He walked her back to their seats.

"Ain't this German pianna player a caution, Margy?" he said. "Wouldn't want to meet him in an alley on a dark night." He glanced around the hall where people were settling into their places. Now there were many empty seats in the once-packed hall. "I wanted to cut out with the other fellows, but my ma would be real mad if I did. She says she paid a lot of money for us all to get culture and if I sneaked out she'd get my pa to tan my hide."

He plopped into his seat in front of Margy and cuffed the brother beside him just on principle. Margy privately thought that it would take more than one Chautauqua concert to "get culture" into the Markers. She sighed. The whole evening was a disaster. What a disappointing end to the Chautauqua visit.

The house lights dimmed as the last people took their seats. Herr Braun reappeared through the side door and mounted the stage. Once more the curt military bow to the audience. Once more the smattering of tepid applause. Once more the heavy curtain with Ben-Hur charging across it rolled slowly up towards the ceiling.

A subdued chuckle swept the audience. There, at the grand piano, his scrawny legs dangling from the bench, sat a little boy running his grubby fingers blissfully across the keys.

Herr Braun's face went a dark muddy red. *"Who this is?"* he demanded, his voice coming from the soles of his polished shoes.

Margy heard several Marker voices in the row ahead breathe "Little Sammy" in one voice. Mrs. Marker, down the line, let out a gasping squawk, but she seemed frozen to her seat.

It was Orlie who was on his feet and up to the stage at a dead run, positioning himself between Herr Braun and Little Sammy, rather like a guard dog fending off a wild animal. Margy, who could not have moved, let alone run up on the stage to confront the ferocious pianist, was filled with grudging admiration for Orlie's decisive action.

Orlie motioned frantically behind his back for his small brother to make an escape, all the while keeping a wary eye on Herr Braun. Little Sammy ignored them both and continued to plink happily on the piano.

"WHO . . . THIS . . . IS . . . ?" repeated Herr Braun in a terrible voice.

Margy could almost hear Orlie's teeth chattering and his voice seemed unnaturally high. "He's my brother, Little Sammy, sir. He don't mean any harm. He just likes pianna music, I guess." Orlie's voice trailed off and he swallowed hard.

Herr Braun brushed past Orlie, marched to the piano and glared at Little Sammy. Little Sammy's cherubic face looked up at him adoringly. The audience held its collective breath.

The face of the great pianist softened slightly. "So, *mein liebchen,* music you like." His voice was suddenly gentle. "How old are you, little one?"

Little Sammy proudly held up five grubby fingers, three on his left hand and two on his right.

"So, *funf,*" nodded Herr Braun. "And what your favourite song is?"

Orlie pushed his way past Herr Braun to stand between him and Little Sammy again. His thin face was so white even his freckles had disappeared. "He don't really talk, Mister. And he don't have a favourite song, not as we know of anyway. Just the songs my ma sings to him at night." Orlie's voice was gradually regaining its natural timbre.

Herr Braun nodded. He edged his way onto the piano bench beside Little Sammy. The small boy continued to stare at him in mute adoration. The audience nudged one another and sat forward in their seats so as not to miss one moment of this astonishing tableau. Orlie stationed himself at the end of the keyboard, close enough to snatch Little Sammy and run if such action seemed necessary.

The great pianist began to play, not the thunderous and complicated music of the first half of the concert, but the gentle lapping chords of Brahm's lullaby. Margy recognized it from hearing her own sweet mother hum it to her long ago in the little prairie farmhouse out west. Her eyes stung with sudden hot tears.

Little Sammy recognized it too. His small hand stole out and stroked the arm of the pianist as he played. When Herr Braun glanced down at him Little Sammy nodded his head and a beatific smile filled his entire small face.

The last lingering notes of the lullaby faded tenderly away. There was a moment of utter silence and then the room erupted into loud and enthusiastic applause. Herr Braun turned on the bench and peered at the audience in a startled manner, as if aware of their presence for the first time. A slow smile softened his stern face.

He turned back to the piano. Setting aside the pile of sheet music stacked on the rack, he began to play for Little Sammy. Margy recognized only bits and pieces, possibly a German folk tune or two, a nursery rhyme song here and there, and once a music box melody. Whatever Herr Braun played Little Sammy smiled and the audience clapped and cheered. Between the pieces people from the back of the room crowded forward to fill the empty seats nearer the front, and some even sat on the floor near the stage.

Finally Herr Braun spoke to the audience. "One more piece of music I play for you. This music I myself have written . . . to remember a beautiful woman . . . *miene ehefrau,* mine wife . . . when our little son is born five years ago, they both together die. . . ."

He turned back to the piano and laid his fingers gently upon the keys. An intense hush fell over the audience.

The music began in hope and expectation, with themes of joy interlaced with those of tranquillity. Then it rose in a mounting crescendo of agony and anger, to subside into wave upon wave of despair. Finally the original theme of hope re-emerged, this time tempered with an underlying tone of acceptance and serenity. The music ended with a single quiet chord, almost like the "Amen" at the end of an evening hymn.

The audience let out its breath as one and relaxed

in its seats. It seemed sacrilege to destroy the moment with anything as profane as applause, and the hush remained unbroken. Herr Braun did not seem to notice, or perhaps he simply appreciated the respectful quiet more than he would have boisterous applause. Little Sammy wiped the tears off the master's face with his grubby hand.

"Now, so," said Herr Braun, suddenly businesslike again. He looked Little Sammy straight in the eye. "I have played. Now for me you will please play."

Orlie was quick to Little Sammy's defence. "He don't play. That is, we don't have a pianna. Little Sammy . . . well, he's a little . . . slow. He don't even talk much, I told you. He just likes music."

Herr Braun ignored Orlie and said again to Little Sammy, "For me you will play." He took Sammy's dirty finger in his hand and placed it carefully in the middle of the keyboard. Then to everyone's astonishment, Little Sammy began with one finger to pick out the tune "Three Blind Mice," slowly and haltingly, but nonetheless recognizable. Herr Braun smiled and joined him by filling in gentle chords on the bottom half of the keyboard to supplement Little Sammy's one-finger effort. The effect was electrifying—on Orlie, on the rest of the Marker family, on the audience. They roared their approval.

When the song was over, Herr Braun said to Little Sammy, "Now then, what I do, you do." He played a simple five-note sequence with one finger: Sammy played it back to him. He did it again with an eight-note sequence. Again Sammy played it back perfectly. Herr Braun got all the way to eighteen notes before Sammy faltered in mirroring them back to him. Then the master played a chord: it took Little Sammy only a moment to duplicate it perfectly. Another chord, and another, and another. Each time Little Sammy played them back to him.

"Is *gut, mien liebchen,*" Herr Braun smiled at Sammy. Then he turned on the piano bench and glared at Orlie. "This boy Samuel is not . . . as you say, 'slow'. This boy is," (he snapped his fingers in Orlie's face), "very talented. Lessons he must have."

Orlie's hitherto white face turned a deep crimson. "But we . . . I mean, my pa . . . like, he don't have money for no music lessons. We don't have a pianna anyways."

"Lessons he must have," repeated Herr Braun.

It was then that The Miracle happened. Margy ever afterwards thought of it as The Miracle of the Chautauqua. Because when Herr Braun said the second time, "Lessons he must have," Little Sammy pulled on his sleeve, looked him straight in the eye and said right out loud in front of all those people, "I got my egg money."

Just like that. *"I got my egg money."* Everybody heard it. Margy was aware that Mrs. Marker let out a muffled scream. Otherwise you could have heard a pin drop out on Hastings Street.

Herr Braun looked from Sammy to Orlie. "Egg money? This I do not understand."

Orlie never took his astonished eyes off Little Sammy, but he managed in a slightly strangled voice, "Little Sammy's chore is to collect the eggs every day. Ma lets him keep one every day and then when he gets a dozen he can sell them for four cents. . . ."

Herr Braun beamed at Sammy. "Is *gut.* 'Egg money.'

Is *gut.*" He stood up and solemnly shook hands with Little Sammy. Then still holding him by the hand, he pulled him from the bench and together they bowed formally from the front of the stage. As one the audience was on its feet, laughing and cheering and clapping.

Then Herr Braun smiled his slow smile, turned and stepped quickly down the three steps and out the side door, leaving Orlie and Sammy alone on the stage. The heavy curtain rolled down but the audience continued clapping and whistling for a long time.

Margy and Aunt Edith told Aunt Alice all about the adventures of the evening when they got home.

"And Auntalice, Little Sammy *talked,* right there in front of all those people," said Margy, her voice going up a full octave. "It was a true miracle."

"Humph," said practical Aunt Alice. "That was no miracle. The only reason the child doesn't talk much is that living in such a crazy household he couldn't get a word in slantwise. The miracle is that he has survived. Now then, we'll just have to be sure that he gets those music lessons. The organist at the church will be glad to teach him, I am sure. I'll speak to her myself tomorrow morning."

But as Margy lay in bed and thought about it that night she was still sure it was a miracle. And what was it Aunt Alice always said, that "miracles always happen in pairs?" What was the second miracle? That Herr Braun who had seemed so mean and distant turned out to be a really good person after all? Or was it that Orlie had run up on the stage to rescue his small brother when everyone was frozen with fear. That was some kind of wonderful too. That showed that Orlie could be brave if he really wanted to badly enough. Maybe someday he would be brave enough to tell everybody what he had done. . . .

And it was an evening she never forgot.

CHAPTER
──12──

I t was all Aunt Edith's fault.

If she hadn't been so picky about the propriety of birthday observances none of it would have happened. Aunt Alice had promised Margy a real party for her fourteenth birthday but because September seventeenth fell on a Sunday that year the celebration had to be postponed for almost a week. Aunt Edith said that a party should *not* be held on the Lord's Day. Moreover, in her opinion, it was tempting Divine Providence to hold a birthday celebration a day early as the person might just up and die before the proper date. (She also never let anyone turn the page on a calendar before the new month started.)

In any case Margy's party had to be put off until the following Saturday. A week can make a big difference to the weather in September. On Wednesday there was an abrupt shift in season. A tremendous all-night thunder storm changed the sultry days of late summer into honest-to-goodness autumn. Aunt Alice made pronouncements about the autumnal equinox and the sun crossing the equator, but Margy was convinced that the Powers That Be were conspiring to ruin her birthday.

She had planned a wonderful outing to Quarry Lake, a "Second Annual Order of the White Cloud Expedition for the Last Official Swim of the Season." Aunt Alice had promised real fried chicken and a cupcake for each of the four members, Margy's to have a candle to blow out.

But Saturday dawned cool and overcast, definitely not swimming weather. Aunt Alice, always ready to make the best of things, suggested a picnic at the "Eagle's Nest." She had wonderful memories of her own girlhood hikes to the top of the Eagle's Nest cliff. Besides, the chicken was fried and the cupcakes were made and in no time, said Aunt Alice, Margy could have her Saturday chores done and be off for a "Fine Outing."

Margy did not share her enthusiasm. She did not like the Eagle's Nest lookout. She had been up there only once, not long after she had arrived in Bancroft, when a group of Junior Fourthers elected to take her up to "see the view." Of course because it had been winter then, they had gone around the long path from behind, and not up the steep front path which was covered with ice. But suddenly there they were, right on the edge of the cliff, looking out across the York River Valley. The others went right up to the brink and admired the view, pointing out landmarks to Margy. She was glad when the raw March wind had driven them all back down the path to level ground, which was more like the comfortable safety of the western prairie she was used to. Margy had never gone back up to the Eagle's Nest lookout again.

But now it seemed that the birthday picnic at the

Eagle's Nest was all laid on. Aunt Alice had spoken to Lenore's mother over the back fence, and to Jane and Cora's mother by telephone, and they all agreed that a picnic up the cliff was a perfectly splendid birthday outing.

Promptly at eleven o'clock the Order of the White Cloud assembled at Margy's Fine House. Jane and Cora brought a bag of licorice whips to add to the party. Lenore brought a well-thumbed deck of cards with only two missing in case they wanted to play Snap. Just as they were about to leave, Verna Cooper came panting up the walk, dragging her small brother Teddy by the hand and glancing furtively around her.

"Oh, Verna," cried Margy, "Are you coming too?" It was the first time she had spoken to her since they had met in front of the Emporium on the day Margy went to Orlie's farm. It was the first time that the Order of the White Cloud had all been together since before the Terrible Incident of the Christmas Cheer money.

"My mother had to go and help our neighbour Mrs. Clarke bake for her sister's wedding," Verna explained in a breathless and rather evasive manner, "and she won't be back until late this afternoon. And Papa and my sisters are all at the Emporium. So I'm looking after Teddy, and I decided that I can look after him just as well at Quarry Lake as at home. So there." Her voice dropped to a whisper. "Jane told me about your party last week, and I knew that no one would see us at the lake so it would be safe for me to come and Papa would never find out. Teddy won't tell," (as if to reinforce this conviction she gave Teddy an affectionate cuff on the ear), "and anyway, I don't care if Papa does find out. I wanted to come."

Margy's joy at having Verna there overrode her misgivings. "Oh, Verna. I'm so glad." She gave her friend a hug. The other three girls were all smiles at having the Club complete again, and Verna grinned back, pleased at the sensation she'd caused.

Cora's face fell. "But we're not going to the lake, we're going to climb the Eagle's Nest." They all looked in dismay towards the small boy at Verna's side. "Whatever shall we do with Teddy?"

The two Aunts came into the front hall just as Cora asked the question. Aunt Alice seemed to take in the situation immediately. If she thought it odd to see Verna Cooper joining the expedition she gave no indication. Still, she looked perplexed.

"I can't keep the child here," she said, "because I have to go down to the library early today. There's a meeting of the Board at eleven-thirty. And your Aunt Edith . . . ." She glanced doubtfully at her sister.

Aunt Edith's returning look clearly declared that she was not going to spend her day tending a four-year-old. "But I've got too much baking to do this afternoon to have a child underfoot and playing around the woodstove. You girls will just have to take him with you. Surely the five of you can keep a good eye on him at the top."

The amiable Teddy, unconcerned at this maze of triple rejection, took two marbles out of his pocket and held them up to the light.

The expedition straggled off. Cora took the lead, a stout stick in one hand and the bag of candy in the other. Next came Lenore and Jane, taking turns carrying the carton of cupcakes which had to be handled carefully so as not to mess the pink icing. After them trudged Verna, dragging Teddy by the hand. And bringing up the rear came Margy carrying the basket of chicken, buttered bread, and milk bottle of lemonade. Bing bounded around and back and forth, circling and weaving and travelling eight times as far as everyone else, in an ecstasy of high spirits.

Margy's own spirits were lower than a garter snake's belt buckle. The basket was very heavy and they had to skirt the long edge of the village so no one would see Verna and Teddy with them and report back to Mr. Cooper. Huh, thought Margy. *Some birthday party.* Yes, it was all Aunt Edith's fault. If they'd gone swimming last Sunday, they wouldn't be heading off to the Eagle's Nest now.

The ascent of the Eagle's Nest was not without difficulty. They went up the village-side path which was much shorter but also much steeper, and made it necessary to pass the box of cupcakes and Teddy back and forth over the straight up-and-down parts. Cora was little help because she simply would not abandon that wretched walking stick, but forged ahead on her own, shouting back irritatingly encouraging comments over her shoulder. By the time the straggling group finally reached the top, the lemonade was well shaken, some of the cupcakes were a little crushed, and tempers were short.

Still, just as they flopped down on the ground to rest from the climb, the sun broke through the clouds and bathed the valley below in a delightful autumn glow. It seemed so different from when Margy had been there the last time, less hostile and frightening, even though the cliff dropped away from their feet with the same dizzying effect.

After a minute or two of silence Margy rallied the troops and took control. Was she not president of the Order of the White Cloud? And was it not her birthday party? And most of all, was Teddy not straying too close to the edge of the cliff already?

"Members of the Secret Order of the White Cloud," Margy's eyes swept the group, "Do we eat now . . . or wait till later? It's not really lunchtime yet, but . . . . Well, we shall put it to a vote."

The vote was decisive. There were no "Nays" and a resounding five "Ayes!" Actually there were five and a half ayes if one counted Teddy who wasn't really a member of the Order but was entirely in favour of eating any time. And to be perfectly precise, it could be said that there were nine and a half ayes, because at that precise moment the heads of George, Snuffy and Ralph popped out from behind a boulder nearby and added their votes loudly. And a second later Orlie Marker appeared up the path. He explained that at this moment his father thought he was scything thistles behind the barn, but he had "escaped" and come to town.

George, Snuffy and Orlie immediately applied themselves to helping Lenore and Jane set out the lunch in a sheltered nook well back from the edge of the cliff. Cora shouted instructions to them and Verna tried to keep Teddy out of the cupcakes until all was ready for the feast.

Ralph drew Margy a little apart from the noisy

group. Not only was he wearing his scarlet braces, but he was carrying a brown paper bag from which he drew the largest box of chocolates Margy had ever seen. It was wrapped in silver paper and had a Cooper's Emporium sticker on it. Ralph thrust it at Margy. "Happy birthday, Margy," he said, his face the same colour as his braces. "Cora told us about your birthday, and when I went to your house to bring this to you, your aunt told me you had come up here. The rest," (he indicated the other three boys with a jerk of his head) "they just kind of tagged along. I hope you don't mind."

Mind! For once Margy was speechless. And at that moment she didn't even mind Orlie. Never had she been given such a gift. The chocolates must have cost at least two dollars. She knew this was Ralph's way of sharing the birdhouse prize without his mother knowing or Aunt Alice objecting.

"Th . . . thank you," stammered Margy. She couldn't keep her eyes off the red braces.

"Thank *you*," he said, "for the swell braces."

"How did you know it was me?"

"Mr. Rainer down at the Hardware Store told me," he explained. "I really like them."

"You don't wear them too often." It was a question, not a statement.

"Only for *very* special occasions. Like the Chautauqua . . . and today."

"What's today?" asked Margy, racking her brain for some important historical event or religious holiday that might occur on September twenty-third.

Ralph grinned. "Today," he said very reasonably, "is

Margy Stratton's birthday."

"Oh," said Margy. It was a very small and faint "oh." Then, nonchalantly, shifting to safer ground, "I thought you figured that Gwennie gave you the red braces."

Ralph shrugged his Ralph-esque shrug. "That's what she tried to let on when she found out how much I liked 'em. But they weren't a Gwennie kind of gift." He looked at her intently. "They were a Margy kind of gift."

Margy was covered in confusion. In fact she could feel confusion dripping off her head and shoulders like melted butter and collecting in a pool at her feet. She was up to her knees in confusion. If only she could think of something cute and offhand to say to Ralph, kind of careless-like . . . .

At that exact moment George hollered, "C'mon you two. Lunch is all laid out. Hurry up!"

Margy smiled at Ralph and cradled the box of chocolates in her arms. "Thanks for the gift, Ralph. I'll keep them forever."

"Sure, kid," said Ralph easily. They joined the others.

The group sat in a large circle around the food. Aunt Alice, bless her heart, had packed a mountain of fried chicken and a whole loaf of bread, sliced thickly and buttered generously. Orlie contributed some apples (quite possibly an involuntary donation from Mr. McAdam's apple trees, thought Margy), and George and Snuffy a bag of somewhat broken oatmeal cookies. There weren't enough cupcakes to go around, but Cora calculated how many bites each person should get in order to be fair. Because it was Margy's birthday, she got a complete one all to herself. Then they each gave her "a pinch to grow an inch."

After lunch they lay on their backs in the stubbly fall grass for a long time, making up stories about the cloud pictures. Snuffy told them a long complicated tale about the Eagle's Nest Point being an ancient Indian lookout, and how a beautiful Indian princess had leapt to her death to save her people. Somehow this didn't quite make sense to Margy but it made a great story.

"Yep," said Ralph, helping himself to another of Margy's birthday chocolates, "I expect that's why St. John's Cemetery is right at the foot of the cliff." He pointed towards the brink. "So that when people jump off, or fall off, or get killed by an attacking eagle, they can just rooooolll them into a grave at the bottom." Everyone laughed.

"There aren't any eagles left," said George. "Just the old nest halfway up the cliff." He pointed authoritatively towards the cliff. "There haven't been eagles here for years and years. My grandfather told me they killed them or drove 'em off after they snatched a little kid. Nope, you sure don't need to worry about eagles any more." He paused and grinned wickedly at little Teddy. "You just need to worry about . . . TURKEY BUZZARDS!" George shouted the last words and grabbed Teddy's leg with imaginary talons. Teddy screamed dutifully and then dissolved into helpless giggles.

They tidied the remains of lunch and wrapped the chicken bones carefully in used waxed paper from the cupcake box. Aunt Alice had told Margy not to let Bing eat the bones as they were not good for him. Besides,

Aunt Edith could make great soup from them next week so they were to bring them home. Then they finished off the rest of Margy's chocolates—everyone declared them "tip-top"—and she put the pretty silver paper box in the pile to take home too. She would keep the *box* forever and put her valuables in it.

Then Cora suggested a game of hide-and-seek. Margy was "It" first since it was her birthday. She covered her eyes and began to count to one hundred. Everyone else scattered. There were lots of nooks and crannies to hide in up there.

Ralph, Jane and Snuffy got "home free" almost immediately and George and Orlie weren't far behind. Margy caught Verna who was hampered in her dash for the safety of "home" by the short-legged Teddy. Cora quite covered herself in glory by climbing a small tree where no one could see her, and Lenore scuttled home free while the rest were searching for Cora.

Now it was Verna's turn to cover her eyes and count. Margy sprinted away from the cliff and crouched behind a wide tree trunk. She held her breath and waited. Why was it taking so long for Verna to call, "Ready or not, you must be caught!" to signal that she was about to start searching? Just as Margy leaned carefully out of her hiding place to check, Teddy's piercing wail cut the air.

"Verrr—na!"

Margy saw Verna's head snap up and spin in the direction of the cliff.

"VERRR—NA!"

The cry came from over the edge of the cliff. There was a muffled pounding as nine pairs of feet ran to the brink and peered over.

There was Teddy, clinging to a small scrub brush which grew out from the cliff about five feet down. Past him were yards and yards of sheer rock face to the level far below.

"Verrr—na, come and get me." The little boy twisted around and looked up, his eyes wide with terror. Verna reached out instinctively for her little brother. She loosed a flurry of shale from the edge that bounced past Teddy and on down the rock face.

"Oh Teddy," wailed Verna, "How ever did you get down there?"

Teddy swallowed a sob. "I was going to hide where it sticks out." He nodded towards a narrow ledge a few feet from his precarious position. "But I slipped." His little face began to crumple. *"I want my mother!"*

Verna was crying now too. "Hang on tight, Teddy," she shouted. "Really tight. I'm going to get help."

She jumped to her feet and took off towards the shortcut path to town. Without a word Cora and George were right behind her. The three disappeared over the edge down the path.

Ralph grabbed Snuffy by the arm. "C'mon Snuff," he said urgently. "We'll try that closest farm at the bottom of the other path. At least we can get a rope." The two boys left at a dead run and vanished among the trees.

Jane and Lenore drew back from the edge, wrapped their arms around each other, and buried their heads in one another's shoulders. Teddy, feeling himself abandoned by everyone except Margy and Orlie, began to wail all the louder.

Margy wiggled flat on her stomach to the edge again and peered over. It seemed a hundred miles to the bottom where the graveyard spread in the tranquil sunlight. She forced her eyes to focus on Teddy's small panic-stricken face.

"Teddy," she said sharply, "Look at me."

Teddy opened his eyes and looked up at her. "Marrr—gy," he sobbed, "Please help me." He let go of the bush with one chubby hand and reached up towards her.

"Teddy," Margy's voice sounded strange in her own ears, as if it were coming from somewhere very far away, "Teddy, hang on tight with both hands. Keep your legs nice and tight around the bush. And don't move."

But Teddy was determined he was going to climb up and shifted his position. Another handful of shale scattered from the base of the bush and bounced down the cliff.

Orlie hissed frantically, "Margy, *do something!*"

Margy pulled herself forward on her stomach and leaned way out over the cliff. She forced herself to speak in a calm and steady voice. "Don't move, Teddy. Verna and Ralph will bring help. I won't leave you until they come back for us." (That is, she thought, unless I faint and topple off of here myself.)

"Margy, I'm scared." The little boy's face was ashen and his voice a whisper. "What if I fall? What if . . . *the turkey buzzards come?*"

"I'm scared too, Teddy. But you've got to stay still. That little tree will hold you fine until help comes." She said this very heartily hoping that it was so. "And there won't be any turkey buzzards." She forced herself not to check the skies around them.

Margy racked her brain for something to distract the child. If he tried to climb from the bush to the ledge he'd fall for sure. The whole cliff seemed to pitch and toss before her. "Listen to me, Teddy," she said urgently. "I'll tell you a story . . . until Verna comes back."

The little boy obediently turned his dirty tear-streaked face towards her, and Margy struggled to think of a story from her childhood that she could remember enough of to keep Teddy involved and concentrating. The Three Little Pigs? No good. Didn't one of them roll down a hill in a butter churn? How about the Little Red Hen then? No, no, no. When the hen needed help, no one would listen to her.

Then Margy heard her own voice begin:

"A bunch of the boys were whooping it up
in the Malamute Saloon . . ."

Slowly at first, and then gradually gaining momentum and conviction:

". . . And watching his luck was his light-o-love,
the lady that's known as *Lou* . . ."

The poem had a hypnotic effect on little Teddy. His eyes got big and round and attached themselves unblinkingly to Margy's face.

"When out of the night, which was fifty below,
and into the din and the glare,
There stumbled a miner, fresh from the creeks,
dog-dirty, and loaded for bear . . ."

On and on went her voice, rising and falling in cadence:

> ". . . I ducked my head, and the lights went out,
>   and two guns blazed in the dark;
> And a woman screamed, . . . and the lights went up,
>   and two men lay . . . *stiff and stark.*"

It was the performance of a lifetime.

> ". . . His eyes went rubbering around the room,
>   and he seemed in a kind of daze,
> Till at last that old piano fell in the way
>   of his wandering gaze.
> The rag-time kid was having a drink; there was
>   no one else on the stool,
> So the stranger stumbles across the room
>   and flops down there . . . like a fool."

Lenore and Jane and Orlie hung over the edge beside Margy in mesmerized attention, even though they had heard her recite the poems at the end of Senior Fourth to complete her Memory Work. But now the poetry had a feeling and an action that it had lacked in Room Six. Now it moved and breathed with drama and emotion. Now the characters lived through Margy's intensity. On and on she went, stanza after stanza. She finished "The Shooting of Dan McGrew" and "The Cremation of Sam McGee," and was halfway through "Dan McGrew" a second time when there was a shout behind her, and a stout rope coiled past her shoulder and looped over the edge.

Ralph's voice said, "Pull the loop carefully around your waist, Teddy, while you hang on with your other hand. . . . That's good. Now, hang on tight. . . ." Moments later Teddy was safe above and they were all drawing back from the edge of the cliff.

Margy let out a long shuddering breath.

"That was a brave thing you did, Margy," said Orlie slowly. "Talking to Teddy and keeping him from moving." Jane and Lenore nodded in mute agreement.

Margy shook her head. "It wasn't brave at all. I was just as scared as scared. I just did what had to be done, just like when you went on the stage after Little Sammy at the Chautauqua concert. That was a brave thing to do, too." She couldn't quite bring herself to say that she was sorry for calling him a dirty rotten coward, because she wasn't sorry.

Orlie looked thoughtful. Indeed the whole group was quiet as they prepared to leave the lookout. They went the longer way back and returned Mrs. Greene's clothesline rope that Ralph and Snuffy had borrowed from the farm at the foot of the hill.

Just as the straggling troop turned onto the main road, Mr. Cooper roared up in his big automobile and Verna, Cora and George tumbled out. Teddy, now that the ordeal was over, broke into a loud wail and wrapped himself around his father's leg. Mr. Cooper, white-faced and tight-lipped, chivvied his two children into his car and sped away in a flurry of gravel without a word to the rest.

They straggled back through town. No need to skirt around the edges any more. Mr. Cooper knew that Verna had been up the Eagle's Nest with Margy.

Jane and Cora peeled off near their house, then George and Snuffy at the corner, and finally Ralph and Orlie disappeared halfway through town in the direction of the Emporium.

In the end it was just Margy and Lenore who trudged up the hill towards the Fine House. Even Bing's tail had lost its saucy lift. They caught up with Aunt Alice at the gate and turned up the walk together.

The Aunts were surprised to see Margy back so soon. And even more surprised to hear Lenore's glowing description of the afternoon's adventures. But pleased. My, yes, very pleased, although they tried not to show it too much.

Aunt Alice said, "There, you see, Margy, how useful it is to have some great literature at your fingertips. Although I must say, I never envisioned you using it in these circumstances."

Aunt Edith sniffed, "Robert Service, indeed," under her breath. But Aunt Alice flashed Margy an understanding look as if to say that, in this case, Robert Service poems were exactly the right kind to know.

After Lenore departed for her house Aunt Alice said, "Margy, you'd better go up to your room and lie down until supper. You look fair whacked."

Margy was glad to do so. She felt "fair whacked." She also needed time to be away from everyone and think for a while about what had happened. Her insides were still turning somersaults.

But only a few minutes later Aunt Alice called her downstairs again. Old Mr. Cooper, Verna and Teddy's father, was standing just inside the front door, turning his hat slowly around and around in his hands. He stepped forward as Margy came down the stairs.

"Margy . . ." He hesitated, then started again. "Margy I just wanted to thank you," he said. "Ralph Phillips says you saved Teddy's life." He swallowed hard and went on. ". . . Saved Teddy's life by talking to him and keeping him calm until they could get back with a rope."

Margy shook her head. "I'm just glad that Teddy is all right, Mr. Cooper." And, she thought, I hope you're not too mad that Verna was even there with Teddy after your saying she couldn't be my friend.

Old Mr. Cooper made no motion to leave. He continued to twist his hat in his hands. Then he cleared his throat and said, as if he were reciting a memorized speech to a large crowd, "Ralph and young Orlie Marker came to see me just now. Ralph told me about today at the Eagle's Nest, but young Marker told me . . . well, he told me what happened last Christmas. He told me what happened to the Christmas Cheer money." Margy stared at Mr. Cooper like one in a trance. What was he saying?

"I'm sorry, Margy. I'm sorry I didn't believe in you. I wish I'd listened to Verna. She never doubted you for a moment. I just didn't understand. I hope you'll allow her to be your friend again."

Margy swallowed. It was the first time an adult had ever apologized to her for being wrong. Mr. Cooper extended his large plump hand towards her and Margy put her small skinny one into it. They shook hands formally.

Aunt Edith looked as if she might just burst into tears at any moment. But Aunt Alice's look was one of sheer triumph, of one long-wronged who has finally been proven right.

Margy said faintly, "What about Orlie?"

"Young Marker?" said Mr. Cooper. "Well, he's owned up. And he knew exactly how much money was in the jar. I told him he can come in Saturdays and work in the Emporium until he earns enough to pay it all back, and the Businessmen's Association will use it to start next year's fund."

"Will his mother and father have to know?" said Margy.

"In a town this size it won't take long for them to hear," said Mr. Cooper. "But he knew exactly what he was doing when he stole the money so he must learn to take the consequence of his actions. I'm going to make sure the Businessmen's Association and the School Board know so that your name will be completely cleared. And I'm going to tell them all about how you rescued Teddy, too."

Margy felt as if a great weight was floating off her shoulders, as though a shaft of golden sunlight was pouring down on her. If her insides had been doing somersaults before, now they were turning cartwheels for joy. But she found it in her heart to feel very sorry for Orlie. Heaven knew what his father would do when he found out what Orlie had done. And what about Snuffy and George and his other friends? It was likely that Orlie's Lonely Time was just beginning.

Mr. Cooper turned to go, then stopped. "About Teddy," he said, this time addressing Aunt Alice, "I wanted to give Margy a . . . well, a sort of reward for helping him."

Aunt Alice drew herself up to her full height. "That will not be necessary, Mr. Cooper. Margy only did what she should have to help out the boy." Her voice held a faint note of disdain.

"Nevertheless," said Mr. Cooper, "I want her to come in to the Emporium and pick out anything her heart desires . . . say, up to ten dollars worth . . . to show my gratitude and make up for my . . . pigheadedness."

Aunt Alice looked doubtful but finally nodded her assent. It was the word "pigheadedness" that did it. That and the fact that they all knew how much Mr. Cooper thought of small Teddy, the only boy after five daughters.

"It's settled then," said Mr. Cooper heartily. "Margy, you come in to the Emporium on Monday right after school. Take all the time you want and look around for something you'd really like. Anything at all."

Margy's eyes were shining. She spoke to Mr. Cooper but she was looking at Aunt Alice. "Oh, Mr. Cooper," she said with a grin so wide it pushed her ears back on both sides, "Oh, Mr. Cooper, I don't need to 'look around'. I already know *EX-actly* what I want."

The author acknowledges with profound gratitude the willing and gracious assistance of the following:

- Mrs. Marguerite Stratton Tennant, who told her the stories;

- Mr. 'Mike' Burns, who provided further colourful detail;

- The *Bancroft Times,* who allowed her into their archives;

- Mrs. MacDonald's Grade Six Class in North Bay, who gave friendship and enthusiastic encouragement;

- Ms. Karen Alliston, Senior Editor at Maxwell Macmillan Canada, whose patient, sensitive and helpful counsel nurtured both *Margy* and *Margy Misunderstood* to completion.

LILIAN LEVERIDGE

AUTHOR OF "OVER THE HILLS OF HOME AND OTHER POEMS."

From "Over The Hills of Home"

+ + + + + + + * + +

Laddie! Laddie! Laddie! "Somewhere in France"
   you sleep,
Somewhere 'neath alien flowers and alien
   winds that weep.
Bravely you marched to battle, nobly
   your life laid down.
You unto death were faithful, laddie;
   yours is the victor's crown.

Laddie! Laddie! Laddie! How dim is the
   sunshine grown,
As mother and I together speak softly
   in tender tone!
And the lips that quiver and falter
   have ever a single theme,
As we list for your dear, lost whistle,
   laddie, over the hills of dream.

Laddie, beloved laddie! How soon should
   we cease to weep
Could we glance through the golden gate-
   way whose keys the angels keep!
Yet love, our love that is deathless, can
   follow you where you roam,
Over the hills of God, laddie, the
   beautiful hills of Home.

                    — Lilian Leveridge.